The BECOMING of Gunther Ferguson

Christina Langford Miller

This is a work of fiction. The events, characters and places are imaginary. Their resemblance, if any, to real-life counterparts is entirely coincidental.

THE BECOMING OF GUNTHER FERGUSON

Published in the United States by
Pintobeans & Cornbread Publishing, LLC
Ohio

ISBN: 979-8-9993801-0-4

First Edition

Dedicated—
To Him whose word
shall not return to Him void,
but will accomplish what He intends
and will prosper in the thing
where He sent it.

Foreword

After more than three decades of teaching creative writing at the university level, I am often asked by former students to read manuscripts that they're hoping to publish. I usually begin such reading with a good deal of trepidation. As a writer myself, I know that how we feel about our writing can be similar to how we feel about our children. No one likes to have their children criticized. And I don't enjoy having to offer such criticism.

However, the other side of the story is that it is a great joy to be able to offer praise and encouragement for work that is well crafted and speaks with a clear voice. I have never offered higher praise to a student than that which resulted from my initial reading of Th*e Becoming of Gunther Ferguson*. In fact, among the hundreds (possibly thousands) of books that I have read throughout my life, this one ranks among the best.

In *The Becoming of Gunther Ferguson*, Christina Langford-Miller has masterfully integrated the physical and the spiritual as well as past, present, and future. Her characters, including the town itself, are developed so that we feel them as real people even as they connect to universal ideas that reach beyond themselves.

Even many of her minor characters have depths of insight and feeling that connect to the reader's experience of life and human existence. She carefully reveals different aspects of her characters' internal lives and previous experiences in ways that fit very naturally into the development of the narrative.

Christina handles huge themes such as the coexistence of good and evil, redemption, and longing both unfulfilled and achieved while never being untrue to the specifics of the story that she is telling. It is rare to see such mastery in a first book. I believe that comes from the life experience that has enabled Christina to write the book. She has seen the good and evil in life, and she has observed how actions in the past can make an impact on the present and the future, even on eternity.

As with any town, there are things about the town of Becoming that you won't like, but once you have visited it, you will not forget it. The story of the town and its residents will draw you in and engage your heart, your mind, and your spirit. And I predict that you will want to visit again.

—Paul Friskney

The Lord has made

everything for its purpose,

even the wicked for the day of trouble.

Proverbs 16:4

PROLOGUE

From the beginning its purpose was clear. Evident in the shape of the mounds that rose on either side of its valley, that if looked at eastwardly and from a distance, resembled the swollen thighs of a birthing mother. From the richness of Becoming's soil, life came forth. A place created for love by love. Created in truth by truth. Fragrant trees and lush blooming things filled its acreage. Leaves rustled applause to their maker and reeds shook with gratitude. Life was important. Life was honored.

Even those things that bubbled up from the belly of Becoming and at first glance seemed to be freaks of nature, one would soon find, if one was watching and listening, to be created to fulfill their own divine purpose, their own special place in the hands of the creator.

But people came to Becoming and began to live in its valleys and niches, dragging across its soil their misdeeds and their shames. Their lies and their humanness. And those vulgar things began to seep into the soil of Becoming and rot it.

But Becoming couldn't be other than what it was created to be. It had to stay true to its truth. God made it. God told it what to be. It couldn't go against God. So it couldn't—wouldn't hold onto the seepage. It had to cleanse itself. And so the rain came and began to wash away the rot.

HATTIE MAE

Nothing big, small, or in between ever got by Ms. Hattie Mae Armbruster—or so it seemed. Every downward look of an eye or brief stolen touch, she rolled into a gold bead and wore around her neck as a memento. Every hushed word whispered between friends in the shadows of an early evening sunset, she pilfered with her itchy ears, turning them into rhymes and chants and singsongs. And every rat's tail flicked behind a rusted out garbage can in some derelict's alley made home, she felt through the stir of the air and remembered. Women in red lipstick and silk nightgowns pulled their shades and drew their curtains trying to keep their business quiet from her in their loud rented rooms. And children with mean words and nasty mouths quieted themselves as they strolled guilt-faced past her house heading towards some new mischief.

In the town of Becoming, Hattie Mae was known as a woman of exceptional senses, recognized for her remarkable talent of seeing all, hearing all, and smelling all. Rumor had it that if she ever died, the real history of Becoming would die with her. The only thing left would be some random dates in a manila folder in the gray, four-drawer file cabinet in the town's Record Department at City Hall.

It was quite by accident that Hattie Mae found that she was endowed with such talent. Of the two houses that were nestled in the cul-de-sac at the bottom of Alpine Lane, hers was painted a sumptuous split pea green. The 1919, two-story house had bubble-paned windows that touched the floors and skimmed the ceilings as they marched around the rooms two by two. Fly-swatted and finger-smeared, they surrendered their uniqueness to become ordinary portals through which Hattie Mae's gift came. The portals in the gee-gaw filled living room were the ones that had the most to do with Hattie Mae's development. Their frames were hand waxed twice a year. Twice per week the glass was wiped with an extra soft cloth—three times if it was a particularly insect-ridden summer. Antique lace curtains hung at the windows, keeping the integrity of the house and making viewing simple. It was here in front of these windows that Hattie Mae skimmed her newspaper headlines, gummed overcooked lima beans and drooled through the early morning hours. It was here, looking up the incline of Alpine Lane that her watching over turned into curiosity of, and her curiosity of became intrusion upon. In the beginning it was because of the good view that she felt called upon to keep an eye on things for everyone while they were off to work, or school, or shopping—whether they had asked her to or not. But somewhere, somehow, things got all twisted up, like things sometimes do. It wasn't long before she forgot the why of what she did, and watching empty humming houses no longer satisfied her. Not when there were lives to be pulled apart and secrets to be vandalized.

But in truth, Hattie Mae was no different from most. She, like others, could quickly be caught up in what her eyes suggested, rarely wondering beyond what was seen to what the truth of something was. And since there was little to be seen next door, she had little interest in pursuing the view from her two dining room windows. The fact that the view only captured a well-maintained, blacktopped drive and several heavily covered windows may have been the thing that discouraged her from further investigation. But if she'd ever taken the time to notice what passed back and forth over that well-maintained drive, she might have found herself having her meals and taking her naps in a different place. And had that happened, today she might have felt the vibrations and heard the sounds, even if only a whisper of them. But she didn't. She spent the day in her usual spot, dutifully shaking her head, moaning, laughing and sighing at the right time while she read her morning paper. Then for the rest of the day she rolled her beads, scratched her ears, sang her songs—and missed it all.

THE CAVERN

The cavern's familiar quiet was gone. In its place a droning exploded through the darkness, flinging itself against the cavern walls and finely pitting the wood surfaces, unassisted and unrestrained. Delving deep into the sand-covered floor it repeatedly returned, blazing and purling over each hard, gray grain. And the man's body shook.

Six-foot, two-inches tall, the man stood dead center in the cavern thumping and pressing at the bulging planks above his head. His face, maple brown and smooth, drew taut. His eyes darted here and there. Every inch of his brown skin wet with the presence of finality. And his thoughts, fragmented by the vibrations, ricocheted away through the darkness.

He had never had such a difficult time focusing in this place, but the droning… It moved inside of him like a thought, but it surrounded him like a voice. But if a voice, whose?

In this place constructed by his own hands, his voice was the only voice he had ever heard. If anyone spoke, they spoke through him. So if not a voice, maybe it was merely a thought—his own thought. Maybe one of those unrecognizable thoughts that makes you snap your head around and wonder where it came from. Maybe that was the reason sweat poured down his forehead and his chest burned like Saturday whiskey.

He touched his nose where thick warm liquid trickled like soup on the chin of a child. A quick sniff sent it hurtling backwards, and with one good hark and a deep swallow, it barely left a taste. Only one drop escaped his parched nostrils and its black redness disappeared into the darkness around his feet.

Without fail, entering the dry hidden place would draw the blood from him. But it was never much, and he was always prepared. For tucked in the rear pocket of his coveralls he carried a large handkerchief. A twelve-year, one hundred percent cotton promise trimmed in hand tatted blue smoke. He tilted his head back and with his forefinger and thumb, gently lifted the cloth out and touched it to his nose. Good. No more blood. Carefully he returned it to his pocket.

Moist or just cold, he had a hard time determining as his gaze followed the bulging ceiling plank from one far end to the other. It wasn't possible that after six months of planning and nearly two years of work the room would develop a leak. Like the ceiling, the walls and floor were sealed concrete covered with waterproofed wood planks. It just wasn't possible. The only bit of light that shone through the ajar door cut across the thickness and slammed hard against his back.

He shifted his position and the light shot out past him creating towering silhouettes and an edge of fear. For the first time since its completion four years ago, he regretted not installing electricity. He concluded that cutting out the bulge, resealing, and repaneling the spot was the only solution. With the abundance of spring rain it wouldn't be smart to wait and then have to suffer with a collapsed ceiling. The dampness would surely destroy all of his hard work of the last few years. None of the Fathers would survive it.

He started for the door as a slow smile crept across his face. "Ah," he moaned. "You know already, don't you?" He waved a long calloused finger at the wooden boxes that neatly lined the walls of the cavern. "Is that what I am feeling down here?" he asked out loud. "Do you know?"

The calming realization left him very impressed with the Fathers. He eased into his usual rendition of the old hymn, "Oh, Lord Will You Remember Me," as he walked.

"Oh, Lord, will You remember me when I am called to go?" He reached the doorway and turned for one final look at the trouble spot overhead.

"When I have crossed death's chilly sea, will He his love there show?" He would have to begin repairs as soon as he finished the work waiting for him in his truck.

"Oh, yes! He heard my feeble cry from bondage set me free." He turned, pulling the door shut behind him. "They'll be here soon," he said softly.

"And when I reach those pearly gates, He will remember me!" Clink. The door shut behind him.

Now standing in his basement, he fumbled around in the top pocket of his coveralls and pulled out the key to the cavern door. There was a tall metal shelving unit that stood just to his left and he laid the key on the very top shelf out of sight.

He rubbed his hand across his chest for what seemed like

the thirtieth time today. The pain had been with him since getting out of bed that morning. Mild and barely noticeable earlier, its fiery fingers now gripped him in such a way as to make concentration on anything else almost impossible.

He could hear his mother's high-pitched screech piercing his ears. "Boy, you ought to know better at your age. You can't eat spicy foods late at night and not expect to pay for it!"

But he had a soft spot for Sister Lula Mae Caldwell's hot chili with peppers, which up to this point had never had this bad of an effect on him. But then again, this was the first time he'd had it since turning fifty-four three weeks ago. He remembered vaguely that the quiet still voice that usually kept him on the right path had told him not to eat it, even while he lifted the first spoonful to his mouth. But, he did it anyway. Yes, he had to unload his truck and get started, but he would have to get some antacid first. Nothing else could possibly help.

On his way to the stairs, he paused at his six-foot by three-foot work table. He patted the stainless steel surface as he did a mental checklist of the room. There was enough bicarbonate. All utensils were clean and ready. There were plenty of jars—he had just purchased several boxes. At last count, there were seven rolls of linen carefully stored in plastic in the drawer underneath the work table. Wood for boxes and sand were good. And the bathing tub was clean. He was ready.

Forgetting to turn out the lights, he made his way to the top of the stairs and opened the kitchen door. He stopped there for a moment to catch his breath. When he regained some energy, he carefully locked the door behind him and padded across the freshly sanitized floor to the sink.

A soft spring breeze blew in from the window carrying with it the smell of budding shrubs and flowers. Just beyond the window, the remnants of multiple small, winter ravished gardens were trying to resurrect themselves.

He closed his eyes and his mother gently stroked his forehead and drew her hand down the side of his arm. He felt her breathing on the nape of his neck and heard her whispering in his ear. For a moment, just a brief moment, his heart stopped racing and the pain in his chest disappeared. But then he opened his eyes and she melted away.

He pulled his wallet from his back pocket and thumbed through it. A life of less need or a needless life, he could not tell. Were they one and the same? "Could you please make it a ten and ten ones?" he had asked of the bank teller the previous week. She nodded politely like she did every other Friday when he would come in and cash his check. Tomorrow would be Friday again. He folded up his wallet with the two-week-old, ten dollar bill and ten ones and laid it beside him on the countertop, giving it one last hard look to remind himself to return it to his back pocket before he left.

The water ran cool from the faucet when he turned it on. He craved it intensely. Thickened pools of saliva were forming in the corners of his mouth. While his left hand monitored the temperature of the tap, he opened the cabinet door with his right.

The rows of tall tea glasses, water goblets and delicate coffee cups on saucers glistened on their yellow lining paper. Without a nick or a smudge, they were ready to be used at a moment's notice. Not that they had in years, though—been used, that is. But they were kept ready because everyone at some time in their life had a visitor or two—didn't they? Not the pretend kind like the ones he would bring up with him from the basement. The kind that did not require a plate, or a glass, or even an eating utensil. The kind with whom he would just nod and smile; and if he asked a question, he would be the one to answer. No, not those kinds of visitors. But instead, the kind who would enter from the front door and at some time during their visit say, "Dinner was so terribly good. May I have just one more helping, please?" Or "This is the best coffee I've had in a long time. Where in the world did you buy it?" Those were the kind of visitors for which the glasses waited.

Four or five large swallows and his own glass was empty. In the bottom of the cabinet where there were neat little rows of various cleaning fluids and garbage bags, he pulled out the dishwashing liquid and shot a dime size amount into the bottom of the glass. While returning the blue bottle to its row with one hand, he swirled the blue dot around in the glass with his other. Adjusting the hot water, he quickly rubbed the glass into bubbles with a dishcloth that hung just inside of the cabinet door. Rinse the glass and then rinse the rag, ring it out and rehang it. Grab the dish towel and dry the glass and return it to its proper place on the shelf. Turn off the faucet and rehang the towel. Now, everything was back in proper order. He turned off the light and slipped through the back door, locking yet another door behind him.

His muddied boots sat in a corner of the deck just outside the kitchen door. He slipped off his house shoes and quickly pulled on the boots while admiring his handiwork. He had built this deck for his mother the year she died. And though she preached constantly about the consequences of a prideful heart, he secretly held himself in high esteem for his self-taught carpentry skills. Small but precise, the deck's corners and edges were perfectly cut. It was a beautiful piece of work. Ten spiraling steps down and he stood on the blacktopped drive that ran from the dead end street to the garage underneath the brick ranch. He looked up at the sky. The rain had stopped. He would have to get to his car out on the street, but first he had to check the garage.

On the rare occasion that he had to leave the house without unloading his truck, he would always check to make sure nothing was visible through the garage window. He had been careful to hang curtains at the two long windows that ran the width of the door. But every now and then, the breeze that resulted from him closing the door between the garage and the workroom would cause the curtains to move ever so slightly, as they had now. But this time not enough for him to go in and straighten them. With an eye against the window he could just barely make out the red Ford truck with its plywood sides. A large brown tarp was draped carefully over the top and tied down at all four corners, and as far as he could tell, nothing was hanging from underneath. He assured himself that he would only be gone for twenty minutes and then headed up the drive.

He slid into the front seat of his Chrysler just as the drizzle began again. He latched on his seatbelt and turned on the radio. "Eleven thirty-five p.m. and sixty-five degrees out. If you're planning on being out tonight, you'd better take your umbrella. It's gonna be a wet one."

"Don't you mean another wet one?" he asked, peering out

into the cloud-filled night. He turned the radio down and settled on the swishing of the wipers to keep him alert. The car moved quietly up the hill and out of the cul-de-sac. Two blocks later he was on the main thoroughfare of Becoming. Once at the all-night drugstore and after several minutes of wading through isles of wintergreen body rub and witch hazel hemorrhoid pads, he found himself standing at the counter searching for the wallet he had reminded himself not to forget. Irritated for being so irresponsible, he had the cashier set his antacid aside and promised to be back in less than ten minutes. But William, the third shift clerk who now at eighty-two was a bit hard of hearing, thought he was told to put it back. And so after he finished restocking batteries on the hooks behind the counter, he walked the antacid back to aisle fourteen where it would remain until some days later when Miss Shannon would purchase it to sooth a stomach distressed by the unseemly goings on under a rained soaked sky. William, always uneasy with the quiet of the third shift, turned up the radio.

"One minute till midnight," announced the radio, "and the rain's still coming."

THE REVEREND CARL MADISON

The Reverend Carl Madison stood at his study window peering through slightly open white slats, ogling the couple two backyards away whose exhibitionist tendencies suited him. It had become for him the eating of the creamy butter mint, the last walking of the dog, the brushing and flossing of teeth—*the after dinner thing.*

As now, the couple's nightly ritual usually took place on the kitchen's rolling island. The woman holding onto the man's neck with her legs locked at the ankles. Her hands like the sails of a boat caught in a frightful wind, whipping back and forth, and up and down. And Reverend's eyes dancing at every unheard sigh and moan.

The man stood, his strained legs anchored in a pool of jeans, and shirt, and boxers—spastic. His large hands cinching his lover's small waist as he mindlessly yanked and jerked at her. And Reverend winced at every thrust of a pelvis and drawing of nails across flesh.

Suddenly, the man threw back his head and Reverend imagined a banshee's cry fleeing the house and getting sucked into the midst of their adjoining yard. His eye twitched and he wondered if they knew he watched.

The feeling of shame that had first made him question the appropriateness of this secret activity had long since disappeared. In its place, a stomach churning regret made him long for the nights he had wasted while at their age. Even now, at this late time in his life, his entire being ached for lost opportunities to count the measure of love by the number of orgasms experienced in one week, in one day, or at one time. He regretted the waste, and he regretted the regret. But at seventy-two years of age, there was little to be done about it.

"Carl? You awake in there?" The voice from the hall nudged him.

Sucking on a tooth, he pulled himself out of the shadows, his face bearing the imprint of flocked wallpaper. From his fingers dangled a red-lined, eraser chewed paper. In not too many hours from now this outline of a sermon would have to guide him in speaking to his congregation with unwavering authority.

His Bible text was Jeremiah 29:11. "For surely I know the plans I have for you, says the Lord." He would have to stand wide-legged and tell his congregation what it meant in their own lives. Commit himself to telling them that lives are planned in the womb—or not. Sing that lives are purposed and they could not help but to live into that destiny—probably.

He did not doubt the strength of his legs and his voice, but his conviction on any of his thoughts remained dubious, particularly since he couldn't get it all reconciled in his own mind.

He understood all of the theological arguments, of course, but he had trouble believing in the absoluteness of any of it.

"Carl? Baby? Can you hear me?"

It was Thursday night already. There was no time left to wrestle with what he did or did not believe. He simply had to come up with something he could preach.

Satan was running him down again, tearing at his lie clothes, mocking his shiny, black walking shoes and jeering at his holy swagger. The chase always left him cold and sweaty in his weed-ridden paths of righteousness.

A sigh, bloated with great hope flared his nostrils as the morning's events played across the window pane. He shuddered in anticipation of what the shadows meant for tomorrow. Today had been the beginning. He was sure of that. It was the beginning of paying the penalty for his sins, and finally, he hoped, the beginning of his freedom.

Sin is such a binding thing.

It was the rain, of course, that started the cleansing and he knew it from the first drop he had witnessed days ago. As if expecting it, he watched expressionless as the first drop landed in front of him. It seemed to say, "Look up! It's time!" It had come down with a robust "ping" into the metal watering can that sat rusted out and dry as a bone on Mrs. Williams' side of the fence as they stood talking one morning. They'd both heard it, and both stared at the watering can as if expecting something to take root and shoot up into the sky from that single drop. When Mrs. Williams finally looked up at Reverend, he could see it in her eyes. She too knew that something was coming—something strange and out of the ordinary.

Then came the cloudbursts. Not just one or two, but a continuous roar. It wasn't until the sixth day or so that Mrs. Williams informed Reverend that she had checked with the National Weather Service and found that there was no reason for such weather events. In fact, there were no thunderstorms showing on their radar at all. They had suggested maybe someone had been running a sprinkler. She had said to Reverend, "I don't recall that being the case. Do you? Do you remember a sprinkler?" When Reverend shook his head no, Mrs. Williams said they should work together to get to the bottom of it. She told Reverend she would start looking everywhere—in her closets and under the covers in her bedroom, while advising all of her friends to do the same to find the thing—whatever it was—that kept the rain clouds hanging suspiciously over Becoming. But Reverend already had his suspicions.

So it wasn't a surprise to him when earlier in the day Becoming's first witness walked up onto Reverend's sit-down-and-rest-a-spell front porch. Sat in Reverend's own rocker grinning and smelling like a piece of rotted meat that had been set back out in the cooler after a quick dip in some bleach water. At first, the conversation was pleasant, remembering days gone by and a time of brotherhood. But soon the witness' words turned sharp and cutting. His purpose became condemning.

Reverend listened intently and watched closely. It wasn't long before he wondered if he would have to pass this trouble on to someone else, just as he did everything else he could not handle on his own.

When the witness left, he promised to return later on in the evening when the night was quiet. And for that reason

Reverend walked over to his desk chair and he sat. He was not sure of the particulars of what he was waiting for, but he knew it was due him. It would be fair and it would be right.

Thunder broke in the distance. It was coming again. He could feel it in his bones.

"Carl, I'm going to bed now. If you can hear me, don't be long, hear?"

THE REOCCURRING DREAM

The sun struck the finely polished bars of the cage and it was brilliant. Brand new and unburdened it sat smack dab in the middle of an intersection during rush hour traffic, perched precariously atop a long-legged, wooden table. The bleary-eyed travelers on either side of it moved in such a slapdash manner that they barely noticed how its impractical placement caused them to have to veer just a little to the left or just a bit to the right. Some drove by slowly giving themselves time to contemplate this fresh new object and wonder at its beauty. Others came to a rolling stop as if they expected to find someone else's misfortune oozing from some large crack in the pavement. Both, however, were mildly irritated that this thing that had caused them to have to rethink where they were going and how they would get there stood empty. One would think that at the very least it should have held something for them to ogle at, point at, particularly since their own cages were so full.

"Reverend?"

Reverend Madison also stood in the middle of the intersection. The wind from the cars whipping his beautiful white silk shirt into the valley between his shoulder blades. He was oddly aware that somehow this cage belonged to him, or maybe even was a part of him. But he never seemed to have time to really think that thought through.

He focused his attention on the familiar passersby. How many times had they come down this road? Always the first, the man with the glinting horn-rimmed glasses, gliding behind the wheel of a mirror-shined black caddy, made his stop. He blinked—once, twice and then three times. The third time was the cue. Exiting the automobile, the man began asking Reverend questions in a language Reverend still could not understand. The only reason Reverend even knew they were questions was because the man would end each flurry of sounds with a guttural "unh?" Reverend struggled the best he could to get some understanding of what the man was wanting from him, but he knew it was pointless. He could not pick out one familiar word or letter that was coming from the man's thin lips other than the consistent guttural "unh." At exactly the same time the men realized there was nothing to be gained by continuing on as they were. So, with one last "unh" and a strong slap to both outside thighs, the horn-rimmed man returned to his vehicle and quickly disappeared into the line of traffic.

Shortly thereafter the mother came with the four children in the back of her car. She slowed down as the man before her had and began pointing out to the children how they should be more like the cage, unoccupied, shiny and clean—clean being the most important thing, of course. Their mother's firm advice caused them all to begin wiping at their sticky candy faces and pulling at their muddied socks. They began pointing out to one another marks and blemishes that needed to be washed away. The mother, when satisfied that all four were repentant enough, hit the gas and off they went. There were several others that passed by and caused Reverend to cock his head with much interest and study. If only he had time to think it through.

"Reverend! Reverend Madison!" With the voice came a mild pain in his left shoulder. The calling was beginning to irritate him. It wasn't time yet.

He looked up. It seemed as if he had stood in the middle of the intersection for hours, but in reality it was only seconds—possibly minutes, but certainly not hours. The clouds were getting darker and were now roaring across the sky. His mouth went dry. It was beginning.

A wisp of some "thing" glided in on the still air above him. Reverend could see the underside of the purest white, soft as chenille wings, and talons. No matter how many times he had stood in this spot, he could never quite get over how beautiful the wings were. They were absolutely alluring. A familiar whisper floated through his mind asking why a creature so small and beautiful would need claws like an eagle. The traffic halted. Reverend could sense that all eyes were now on him. He wanted to look away to see what they were staring at but couldn't. "Why weren't they also watching the wings," he wondered? Grand shadows seesawed across his face and over the heads of the men, women and children who were now standing outside their vehicles watching him—considering him. Reverend pondered what the expectations were. He concluded that they were waiting to see if he would allow the wings to enter the cage. In his mind he began a conversation with the wings. "You are far too beautiful to be of any harm. You couldn't possibly soil the cage. What would you want with such a small space anyway? Would you be there forever if I let you in?" Reverend pondered the questions along with answers and consequences of action. While he was still thinking and still undecided for the briefest moment he took his eyes off the wings and lifted the latch of the cage door. That was all it took. The wings swooped down, brushed against his sleeve and pushed through the narrow opening. It was in. "Oh, Lord," he thought, feeling the first inklings of panic rising in him. "What have I done?" Reverend spun around. The travelers were pointing at him—gesturing at him—shaking their heads in an "I told you so" sort of way. Whoops of excitement filled the air. They were cheering and he understood it to be because he was now one of them, although he didn't know what that meant.

The people returned to their cars and moved along their way as he returned his attention to the cage. Startlingly beautiful, the wings quivered and fluttered but ever so lightly so as not to be a disturbance. They pinged against the dainty bars as talons rose up and down on a remembrance of pink bubble gum Reverend used to blow to baseball size as a child. Still, all he could see were the wings and talons. Reverend strained to see the other side of the wings as it finally came to a standstill, but his feet were so firmly planted that he could not move around the cage. So he waited. It inhaled and stretched upward, coming to rest on the full length of one of the bars. The anticipation was so exhilarating that Reverend had to remind him-

self to breath. And then suddenly without warning it whipped its head around with a smirk that sent chills up Reverend's already tingling body. Reverend suppressed the urge to scream. He reached out and slammed the cage door and heard the metal crash together. But it had been so beautiful outside the cage. The latch rattled lazily and his mind whirred on. Chunks of peeling dead skin hanging in shreds on a face that looked like his sat atop the wings. Reverend felt betrayed. Jutting its neck out at the onlookers the man-bird batted at them like some street corner hussy, at times daring them to notice, and then at other times inviting their looks. But at all times it was clear from its expression that resting in the belly of the cage rendered it wholly satisfied. Why didn't they notice how horrifying it had become? The air above him began to stir and Reverend looked up in horror. There were more of them gliding above him. But even from above they were not so white and not so beautiful. In various shades of gray and black they circled above him on contorted wings. Still unlatched, the door of the cage eased itself open once more and soon another one landed on the bar and hopped in. It called out as if announcing itself or asking if there were room for one more. The first called back as if to say there was plenty of room. They fluttered at each other momentarily before nestling in with their backs to Reverend and nudging up against one another. Proudly they nested in their new found space, anticipating the coming of more like them. Once the second one came it was easier for the third and the fourth and so on and so on. One after another the grisly creatures flew into the cage announcing themselves and settling in. Each new entrance began a fresh beating of appendages, along with a silent profession of a right to enter. And then propping itself up firmly against the last one before it until there seemed to be no more room. Eventually, they had pressed in so tightly that the seams of the metal cage were compromised. They settled into a cooing that was soft and steady. Reverend felt his breathing fall into the rhythm of their breasts rising and falling. But not long, and their contentment began to wane. Suddenly they were pecking and screeching and slamming up against one another. Reverend pushed at the door trying to keep them in and others out, but the bars were now bent and the door would not latch.

"Reverend! Reverend Madison! Wake up now!"

Reverend's fear was choking him. From top to bottom the creatures squeezed and pushed until finally he could not hold it any longer and the door burst open. Surprisingly, the creatures did not immediately leave. They seemed to be taunting Reverend, taking pleasure in his fear. He was the one who had allowed them in. If people were still watching, and they were, what would they say? What would they think?

The first one to leave hopped on the bar at the door watching Reverend and then suddenly lunged, pecking and squawking at him. Reverend tried batting at it to force it back into the cage, but a second one flew out and then a third and then they were all screeching and striking at him. Reverend flailed and punched as they pecked at his beautiful hands. Spots of black gooey liquid turned to crimson blood dripping down his arms, down his pants and over his shoes. His beautiful, beautiful hands. Would they ever be clean again?

"Reverend Madison! You wake up now, I tell you!"

Reverend's eyes popped open as he jolted straight up in his

bed, leaving his figure outlined in sweat on the pale blue sheets. He fanned vigorously at the fading shadows of the birds as they burst from their wire cage and flapped furiously after him.

"You're dreamin' again, Reverend. Can you hear me? Are you woke?"

His heart was beating too fast for him to answer. He turned to Ruth trying to listen. Woke? Had he been asleep? Realizing his arms were high in the air, he lowered them, folding them across his torso.

"You woke, Reverend? Answer me now!"

Reverend nodded his head as best he could and tried to get reoriented.

"Reverend, I done told you, you need to see somebody."

"Um." Thunder cracked off in the distance and he looked up just in time to see lightening dash across the sky. He was exhausted. This time he had been swinging so hard that both forearms ached. For as long as it took him to gain some strength back, he sat listening to the rain. "You lie back down and finish resting," he finally said patting Ruth's heavy thigh. "I might as well try to work on my sermon while I'm awake."

"I swear, one of these nights you're gonna have a heart attack. You alright? Look at you, you're drenched. Get up and change your clothes," she said pushing at him. He threw his legs over the edge of the bed and they wobbled beneath him as he crossed the room. He pulled his robe down from the bedroom door hook. Ruth turned her large frame over and settled back under the quilt.

"Birds flapping outta cage. Something's wrong somewhere," she fussed. "It ain't normal to be dreamin' that every night."

"Not every night," he thought to himself, "just most."

He pulled the door quietly behind him as he stepped into the hallway. With a hand on the wall to steady him, he made his way along. Beyond the door he could still hear Ruth fussing, "Birds flying outta cage! What in the world? Man I done told you that you need to see somebody about that."

For the twelve years he had pastored the Promisekeepers' Church, he had lived here with Ruth in the church's adjoining house. He knew every crack and dent in the plastered walls and every creak and whine in the hardwood floors, just enough information to maneuver his way towards his office without further disturbing either.

His office was behind the kitchen so he stopped at the refrigerator to find something to help quiet his nerves. Leftovers from the past week's meals were lined neatly in Tupperware containers on the three shelves. Ruth was a good cook and it made him appreciate how long it had taken him to finally marry. No spending years of being practiced on and hoping she would become a good cook. He did not get her until all the practicing was over. But he knew for a fact that he would have been happy to have her anyway she came. He knew he did not deserve her, and he was sure glad to have her. At this time in his life it would be lonely if she was not there to share life with. Hiding behind a bowl of fresh green beans Reverend found the remnants of a sweet potato pie. There was nothing he loved more and nothing Ruth fixed better. They were a perfect match. "Just what I need to settle my nerves." Reverend closed the refrigerator and unwrapped the pie in the dark on the counter and pulled a fork from the drawer.

A light from a nearby window kept his knees safe from furniture edges as he made his way to his desk. He had only been gone from the room for a few hours, but the chair squeaked at him as if he had been gone a week. He had sat there long past bedtime waiting as promised for the witness to return. But he never did. It was with unease that he hoped there had been a change of heart and the return visit would never happen. For a while he sat in the dark eating his pie and pondering it all, the visit—the nightmare. The visit was unexpected. The nightmare had been a regular occurrence in his life. They had just come more often since moving back to Becoming.

Sucking down the last forkful of pie, he looked longingly at the bottom of the metal container. A sound from the kitchen startled him. He pulled open the right-hand bottom drawer and sat the pie pan down on his topical Bible, hoping that if it had been Ruth he heard, she would not recognize the guilt on his face. Lord only knows what or who she was saving the pie for. He looked across the desk at the clock. It was ten minutes till six, an hour and ten minutes until he had to be at the church. He waited quietly for a moment until he was sure Ruth was not stirring. The already open drawer drew him, and he stared at its back compartment. Although what he kept there was not in need of so much space, at one time he did feel it needed its lock. But having been with Ruth for so long, he had learned to trust her implicitly, so that now, using the key was only from habit. Still, he knew that if Ruth did take a notion to look one day, things would never be the same. Somewhere in the back of his mind he believed—knew—the item in the compartment had something to do with the birds, but was not yet able to admit it. Because in admitting it, he would then have to do something about it. Lately, he had found himself opening the compartment almost daily, just as he was now. He switched on his desk light and fumbled for the key in the far back corner of the top drawer. Bending with a tired effort, he unlocked it. The familiar tattered photo lay exactly as he left it with a corner sticking just inside one of the side joints so that he could always tell if it had been moved. Of course, it had not. Switching on his desk light, he reached in and pulled it out, holding it under the light for a better view. As he had for so many years he stared at the young woman in her heavy heels with the black patent leather pocketbook draped across one arm, holding onto the hand of the little boy at her side. The young boy was looking up at her adoringly—admiringly. Reverend's stare deepened, until eventually he was looking at things that most others would never have seen in the photograph. Things like guilt and accusations. And lately, even blackmail. And as he had for so long, he wondered at the thoughts of the woman and the innocence of the child until he could stand it no longer and returned them both to the back of the drawer.

COOKE

Before there was Jesus, there was Cooke—at least in Reverend's life. Reverend's own burden carrier and sin bearer. A stubborn and wiry man, Cooke stood five foot ten with a complexion that could shame Satan's lies.

Sloshing through the morning storm darkness in the courtyard between house and church, Reverend could hardly contain his anxiousness to see his cousin. He and Cooke shared the acquaintance of the witness who had come knocking on Reverend's door the day before. And, of course, Reverend had called Cooke as soon as it had left his office. He'd shared with him what they had said to one another without omitting one single solitary word. Not one thing had been left to Cooke's imagination where Reverend was concerned since the day they fled Becoming together years ago.

The door Reverend entered from the courtyard was the back door to his office. He shook himself off on the felted mat and left his umbrella and overcoat in the small cloak area. The sparsely clad room had not been changed since the previous owner's demise. Somewhere inside, Reverend was certain that eventually someone would enter the room, point an accusing finger at him and say, "The jig is up. Gotta go! Gotta go!" So, the less decorating, the less attached he would be to the space. The less attached, the easier to leave.

He sat down in his chair behind his desk and did a quick survey. On a normal day, his attention would first go to the urgent things. Hospital visits and pressing paperwork. But today would have to be different. Ruth was right. He did need to see somebody. He needed to see Cooke.

A momentary distraction, Reverend pushed back in his chair and smiled, what would unknowingly be his only smile of the day, as he reached for the tower of peppermints sitting on the corner of his desk. The mental image of its creation wrote itself into his Sunday sermon.

"Count the mints Bertha." Sister Janie Johnson stood peering over Bertha Pearson's shoulder, pointing a white gloved finger at a glistening crystal bowl whose lid had been laid aside while the Pastor's Committee attended to their mission.

"One, two, three..."

"Well? How many in there?"

"Would you hold on a minute! I can't count with all you rushing me." Two of the other four women moved in even closer poised to help count if need be.

Bertha began again. "One, two, three..."

"Did you bring the bag Ernestine?" Janie whispered trying not to interrupt the counting.

"Yeah, got it right here!" Ernestine lifted the bag up so that it could be seen.

"Okay! There's twenty-four in here," said Bertha confidently. "There should be twenty-five."

"Yes, twenty-five!" echoed the group.

"Twenty-five for sure. That's what's in the book. Twenty-five."

"Give me one out the bag, Ernestine," demanded Bertha sticking her freshly vaseline-shined palm out.

And on top of the twenty-fourth, she laid number twenty-five. Then synchronously, the women folded their hands, released their furrowed brows and sighed a deep contented sigh.

It was thoughts like these that made Reverend consider that maybe everyone did have a place to fill. Maybe everyone was created for a purpose—even to accomplish the simplest of tasks.

Reverend pulled a business card from his shirt pocket and thought about the purpose of the witness—Kevin Kelley. The business card was from the only motel in the small town of Becoming where Kelley was staying. Reverend had a hard time believing he had once called this man a friend. Someone with whom he and Cooke had shared an apartment, food, and many hard times. But if anyone knew, Reverend knew that time could change a person, sometimes for the better, sometimes for the worse. And as for his old friend Kevin Kelley, it had definitely been for the worse.

"Bring me the money tomorrow, or I'll have to visit your church on Sunday and let your members know just how far back we go."

Reverend looked up at the clock stuck in the steeple of a hand-carved church plaque. People would soon be coming. He had to get down to the kitchen before breakfast began.

In the community hall, the air smelled of lack, singed toast from day old bread and thinned coffee. Reverend stood opposite the kitchen watching and listening to mercy's voice. Old metal legged classroom chairs screeching across a tiled floor, plastic spray bottles under the hands of community volunteers shish shishing watered down bleach across Formica topped tables, and the thumping of a kitchen knife on the kitchen counter.

In just a little more than an hour the doors to the dining hall would open and in they would come. From the sanctuaries of bridge and overpass footings, abandoned buildings and alleyways, no name-no face folks would enter the room filling it with poor smell, challenging even the most sympathetic of workers to stay in the room for any length of time without having to take a break to inhale.

"Hey, Reverend!"

Reverend turned to his right just in time to see the glint of a gold tooth disappearing behind a pair of full, mottled lips. Hobbling towards him on a cane was Deacon Jasper Williams. He approached Reverend with an outstretched hand and as they shook, positioned himself at Reverend's side.

"Are those eggs I smell this morning, Brother Deacon?"

"Yessuh, yessuh," he replied, running his hand across a sparsely populated gray afro. "Haven't had 'em in a good while, but the Lord sure blessed us this morning."

"Good. I believe they'll be some happy folks in here shortly. Everything else going as well?"

"Well, not so much." His eyes followed the hubbub in the dining room as he spoke. "That, uh, uh… What's that fellow's name?" He thumped his temple with his finger. Reverend waited patiently knowing that any attempt to help would be useless. Deacon poked toward the exit door and then the kitchen a couple of times. "Oh, yeah, that's it! Brother Ferguson. He ain't showed up yet. Got everything a bit off schedule."

"Oh?" Reverend checked his watch. "I don't know that he's ever been this late. At least not without calling. But maybe he's waiting for something at one of his pickups. He wouldn't be late without a good reason."

"Well, maybe so. They're in there using the fruit and stuff they had left over from yesterday. Lucky thing we got those eggs from Bancroft Farms last night. Least they got something else they can serve with them oranges and burnt toast if he don't show up soon."

A mild pang of concern swept through Reverend. If nothing else, Gunther was constantly and consistently punctual. At exactly six o'clock every morning he would come by the church and unlock the doors for the workers. By six fifteen he was headed to the three vendors on Roe Street that donated day old goods for the sixty or so people they fed in the hall each day. Reverend stuck his hands deep into his pockets and jiggled his pants legs trying to rid himself of the uneasy feeling that was riding up his leg.

"You sure he hasn't called?"

"Not as I know of he ain't."

"Well, then, I'd better go see what I can find out. Oh, and by the way," he asked over his shoulder as he walked away, "Have you seen Cooke this morning?"

"He was on his way out back to his garden last time I seen him. Something he needed for his lunch soup." A hand over his head was Reverend's sign of appreciation as he continued towards the kitchen. Deacon's untrusting spirit always found place at Cooke's feet. Day in and day out he would go on and on about "that mess that man was back there growing. And y'all eating it up like slop. None a y'all knowing what it is. Could be that marjuana or anythang."

Inside the kitchen the thomping had stopped. The culprit, a dull brown handled knife, lay on the counter in a splash of orange juice speckled with seeds. Beside it sat a large silver tray filled to overflowing with typical cafeteria dessert bowls—the white china type with a thin green ring circling the edge. Inside each were two quarters of a precisely cut orange.

At the moment, Julia Lewis stood at the kitchen island scratching burnt toast.

"Good morning, Ms. Lewis."

"Good morning, Reverend," Julia answered without looking up.

Reverend walked by noticing her without staring. He'd always thought her a very handsome woman. Fine cut features and delicate but firm hands. Still young—only in her forties. There was a rumor in Becoming that as a young teen her father had gotten her pregnant and she went off somewhere to have the baby. The story was never confirmed, but it would certainly explain her disinterest in men and her solitary life.

Out on the church's covered side porch Cooke was sitting on the edge of a brick wall fingering a pot of basil. A portion of the church that had long since lost its usefulness, Cooke had turned the space into a potted garden. Mostly he had planted herbs, but in the summer there were a few extras like tomato plants and greens.

"Where is he, Cooke?" Reverend pushed the door up behind him.

In fluid motion, Cooke glanced up barely acknowledging Reverend and then went back to picking at his pots. He took his time answering. "D-d-don't know. Guess he's s-s-somewhere loading his truck."

"I'm not talking about Gunther." Reverend noticed Cooke's stammering seemed to get worse with age. He stood firmly in front of Cooke and crossed his arms. "He didn't show up last night like he said he would."

Cooke paused briefly, seeming to give more thought to Reverend's question. "Aw, you mean…"

"Yes, I mean Kevin Kelley." Just saying his name and the witness' figure seemed to loom over Reverend. "What happened to him?"

"Now, how in the hell would I know? Besides, I would think you would be happy he didn't show up. The man left you with a peaceful house. No explaining to be done to that sweet wife of yours. You can spend today like you do every other day, healing the sick and raising the dead!" Cooke swept his arms up to the sky, ended with one loud "Ha!" and then chuckled quietly.

"Cooke, I just want to know if you have any idea why he didn't show up."

Cooke's whole body suddenly went quiet. He stood up to face Reverend eye to eye. "What do you think I did?" he whispered, looking around as if expecting someone to be listening from one of the windy corners of the porch. "You think I took that man out in the woods somewhere and wrung his neck? Laid him out there for the wolves to find him? You think I offed him, Reverend All High and Mighty?"

Reverend felt the blood rising in him. "I didn't say anything of the such, Cooke." He pulled a handkerchief out of his inside coat pocket and ran it across his forehead.

"Then don't be questioning me old man," he replied coolly. And then he just stared—stared until Reverend dropped his eyes. He turned his gaze back to his herbs. "You always wanting me to do your dirty work so you can stand back all sanctified and holy and ask me about what I did."

"I just want to know that you didn't do anything stupid."

"Now you callin' me st-st-stupid?"

"I ain't calling you stupid, Cooke. For crying out loud! Why you always got to turn things around?" Reverend turned his back and took a few steps away.

"Why you always got to be in my face, man? You always trying to run my business."

"Run your business?" Reverend snapped around.

"Yeah! Run my business! When you called me it became my business," he said with a thump to the chest. "And don't stand there and pretend you intended anything different. We may be older, but you ain't changed. Now, if you want it b-back, just say so."

Hurt, Reverend watched on in silence as Cooke sat back down on the wall and returned to his pots. He could never figure out the root of these arguments that would leave Cooke angry and him hurt and feeling guilty. He took a few more steps away from Cooke, nervous about having to approach the next subject.

From under the awning the rain had slowed down to a light drizzle. The gray-black clouds hung heavily in the sky.

"Gunther hasn't shown up yet," he finally said, speaking out into the universe as if it had an answer for him.

"Dammit, I know that. And?" The edge had left Cooke's voice. With herbs neatly sorted in an old plastic butter container, he stopped pulling up thyme and stood up.

"They're starting to get worried in there. It's not like him to just not show up," explained Reverend.

Cooke brushed the dirt from his hands and pants while he tried to straighten his seventy-five-year-old, stiff body. "I'll drive over to his house. Maybe he just overslept. He put in a long day yesterday." Suddenly the door to the kitchen slammed. They both swung towards it. "You need to be more careful with your doors."

"You think someone heard us?"

"How would I know, you ol' fool." Cooke picked up his sprigs and they both headed inside.

"I'll go out to the farm to see if he's out there." As the words were coming out of his mouth, Reverend knew he should have just gone without announcing it.

"He better not be. I told him to stay off my property. He's just encouraging all those vagrants to hang out there. If they're hungry, they can get here like everyone else does."

"Some of 'em too old, Cooke."

"I don't give a damn. They hungry and begging. They need to come to the food. We ain't a delivery service."

With Cooke on his heels, Reverend headed back to the kitchen. "Sister Julia? Is everything okay in here?" This time Reverend shut the door behind him.

"Sorry, Reverend—Cooke. I'm just trying to get all of these bread scrapings up from the floor. I guess I hit the door with the broom, and with the wind and all, I guess it slammed. Sorry."

The two men stepped over the crumbs.

"Don't be in here making a mess in my kitchen," fussed Cooke. "This is a kitchen, not a city dump! I've got an errand to run. By the time I get back, you all should have things ready." Cooke laid his herbs on the cutting table and pulled off his gardening gloves.

Reverend headed to the door looking at all the bread crumbs on the floor near the door. He decided not to ask Julia how the crumbs had gotten there when the cutting table and the garbage cans were both on the other side of the room.

HIGH YELLA PEOPLE

"G—g—g—go around, then, st—st—stupid!" Cooke's tongue willfully clicked at the roof of his mouth. Just once, even today alone in his car, he would have liked to experience his anger without this sissified distraction.

He looked up at the high yella, just like Reverend's face, woman in his rear view mirror. She'd been riding his tail since turning onto Beekman Street, two panhandlers and one bar ago. Her impatience, though justified, spiked his meanness—his *kiss-my-assness*.

He slammed an arthritic fist against the steering wheel. Without a doubt, he believed light-skinned wenches always thought they could flash a buttercream smile or shake their high yella hips and sweet kisses would be planted on their high yella rear ends. And then the world would assure them that anyone or anything causing a bump in their otherwise creamy yella road would immediately be run over. But not today. He was the front runner on the yella brick road today. And she would just have to be satisfied to ride behind him doing twenty-five miles in a thirty-five mile per hour zone.

Pinned between Cooke and a bus on her right, the woman leaned on her horn—magnificently. Once, twice, three times. Finally they reached a red light. She stuck out her head and yelled obscene driving orders through the rain to Cooke.

"What the hell's the matter with you old man!" screamed the twenty-something-year-old. "Why don't you just get out and walk?"

Finally the light turned green and Cooke pulled out. The bus remained at a standstill giving the woman an opportunity to whip around to Cooke's right side. For a few moments, he pretended not to notice her, but then his adrenaline kicked in. When he could contain it no longer, he rolled down the window, rain splattering his velour seat.

"Meet me in hell you w-w-wench!" Then off he sped, his foot mashing the gas pedal to the floor.

Dealing with Reverend was getting harder and harder the older he got. And, it was getting harder and harder to keep secrets and find other ways to release his anger. But this was good. This event so exhilarated him, he could just pee. Pee all over himself.

Before he knew it, he was turning the corner of Alpine Lane, following the rolling curb water down to the bottom of the cul-de-sac and pulling into Gunther Ferguson's driveway. He stepped out onto the blacktop.

There was no car or truck to be seen from the top of the driveway. Gunther was a creature of habit, and when he was home, his car was always parked at the top of the driveway. Always.

Cooke rang the doorbell several times and no one came. He headed to the back of the house.

"He ain't home!"

Cooke was so startled he slipped and nearly fell. When he finally stilled, he turned towards the direction of the voice.

"What? What you mean he ain't home?"

"He ain't been home since last night."

It took him a minute, but he eventually caught a glimpse of two eyes peeking from behind a curtain in the window across the driveway. He'd been back in Becoming long enough to know about Hattie Mae. Everyone did.

"Well, how you know he ain't here."

"Don't take no genius to see his car ain't here."

"Could be in the shop," he said under his breath, and then added, "you nosy biddy."

"I sawed him when he pulled off a little after eleven yesday e'ning. Now, like I said, he ain't home!" Her final words were punctuated with a snap of the curtain and suddenly she was no longer visible. Cooke stood for a moment in the drizzle trying to decide if going around to the back was worth the effort, then decided it certainly was. He needed to know for himself that Gunther was nowhere on the premises. Slowly he maneuvered himself down the sloping blacktop. He reached the back and began to call as he started up the deck steps.

"Gunther! Gunther! You up there?" He looked out into the misty yard filled with one dead winter worn garden plot after another. Ice burned stems connected to brown roots heaved from the saturated ground. He made his way up the deck steps. "Gunther! You in there?!" Three more times he called out and banged with no response. Peering through the door window into the kitchen, he could see that the lights were all out. Not so much as a shadow or a fly fluttered around. And as usual, nothing seemed to be out of place. Not even a cup on the counter. He turned to head back down the steps but something inside caught his attention. He turned and pressed his nose up against the glass. It was hard to tell and his eyes weren't as good as they used to be, but it appeared to be Gunther's wallet. Just a tip peeking out from behind the refrigerator on the counter.

"Surely, Gunther, you wouldn't have gone somewhere without your wallet. Course, you could have forgotten it, I reckon, but… Or could be you bought a new one and was getting ready to throw that one out."

If he wasn't nervous before, he sure was getting there now. He turned and headed down the steps. "Ole biddy," he muttered as if Gunther's nosy neighbor was the cause of him not being there, simply because she knew he wasn't.

He walked around the blacktopped area at the bottom of the steps and peeked into the garage. Just a corner of the curtain was raised and he was able to see a sliver of Gunther's red truck parked inside. The chilly wind blew a foul smell past Cooke and he coughed it away. "Well, if he's in there, he's either asleep or dead. And if I'm not careful, I'm gonna catch my death of cold out here." Cooke shuffled his way back up the driveway and made it back to his car. One more careful look in each window of the house, and he pulled out of the drive and headed back to the church's kitchen.

THE ROCKING MAN

Reverend teetered on the edge of Becoming watching steam rise from the ground and snatching memories back from a black hole of forgotten things. His nose flared as the scent of wet earth filled his nostrils.

His elbow was perched on the cream-colored, leather armrest of his Cadillac. He leaned heavily like big, rimmed-hatted men sometimes do, staring out of the rolled down passenger side window. Several yards ahead, the 1892 ramshackle of a house demanded of him a look. He had driven by it and driven to it. And even gone inside as recently as two months ago. But it had been a long time since he had looked at it. Seen its despair. Noticed its failing roof and sagging window sills. Wondered at the missing porch railings mimicking the gap-toothed, homeless folk it now housed.

The house technically belonged to Cooke. Their grandmother had left it to him in her will. But for his own reasons, after a few years, Cooke chose to move into the church's basement. Momma O, or Black Olive as some of the town folks called her, had raised Cooke here, and even though he was living in Chicago at the time, she thought him the logical choice to carry on the legacy of caring for the needy from the back porch. Only Cooke didn't see it that way. And once he seemed to finally wash his hands of the place, Gunther stepped in.

The property sat almost an equal distance between Gunther's last pickup of produce and the church. It had become Gunther's habit to stop by the property first to make sure that those who couldn't or wouldn't make it to the church had food for the day. Reverend had known of the habit for a long time, but both men knew it wasn't a good idea to tell Cooke, considering his dislike of what he called bottom feeders. Reverend stepped out of the car.

There were memories here. Memories that smelled like wildflowers and tall grass, and felt like bare feet on a cool dirt road. Sounded like crickets in the night and roosters in the morning. Tasted like fresh lemon pound cake with homemade ice cream and blueberries. And looked like dusk, firefly lit in wide open spaces. There were memories here.

He moved across the yard through the drizzle remembering the first trip here as a thirteen-year-old. His mother crossing and uncrossing her legs and folding and unfolding her hands during the train trip. A tenseness that he still did not understand filled the air when he stepped out of the taxicab with her and stood waiting for the grandmother he'd never met to say something—anything—from her perch five steps up on the wide, breezy porch. And he remembered his sixteen year old cousin Moses, who he would soon come to call by his nickname *Cooke*, appearing out of the thick air suddenly beside him saying, “Well, you gonna stand there forever? I been waiting all day to go swimmin’.”

The house was in a dire state of disrepair. Shutters hung askew, windows were broken and bare. While Cooke had grown up here, he’d only been to visit on three occasions as a boy. But each of the visits held powerful memories. Reverend walked through each room, standing for a moment hearing the voices of the past. In the living room there was a pallet of old newspapers and an old torn blanket. Someone was sleeping here and Reverend wondered if it was one of the people he had passed standing at the door of Promisekeepers.

He’d spent a lot of time in the kitchen with Cooke. That was where his cousin had convinced him that opening a restaurant together would be advantageous to them both. He with his cooking skills and Carl with his keen eye for business. They’d agreed in that kitchen to begin their journey when Carl graduated high school, and hands were shook.

The upstairs was worse than the down. Reverend’s foot almost went through one of the risers on his way up. Somewhere at sometime there had been a leak and the floor was rotting through. In Cooke’s old bedroom, the beds were still in the same place they had been the last time he had visited. He remembered nights where sleep came late because the conversations they had drew long. He also remembered the time when there was a silence so deep his thoughts echoed back at him. He stood there for a long time remembering that silence and realizing that was when those times of guilt and anger became a part of their relationship so many years ago.

He’d been so intently remembering that he was startled

when he finally looked down through the bedroom window and saw someone sitting on the side steps. Their foot was propped up across one knee and they were carefully and steadily picking the dirt from between their toes.

The sight drew a hint of disgust across Reverend's face and he fought with his desire to just continue remembering—remembering his second visit here racing across the yard with wild excitement, searching for his cousin, now best friend. Barely slowing down as he planted a kiss and gave a closed-eyed hug to his grandmother before running through the house, yelling, "Moses! Moses! Where you at?" He could still hear his feet on the hardwood floors, click, click, clackiting in his we going somewhere special shoes. Shoes very much like the ones he wore today, only now his feet moved much slower.

He made his way back outside and reaching the steps, he grabbed hold of the railing on the opposite side of the visitor.

"Hello?" Up close, the man looked to be in his late sixties or early seventies. When his greeting went unanswered, Reverend had to weigh whether it was because the man was hard of hearing or simply disinterested. So he settled on speaking louder.

"It seems everyone must have gone to the church for breakfast. Is there a reason you're still here? Are you waiting for someone to come take you?" Reverend knew it was a stupid question, but he never was the best at talking to the homeless.

The man finally looked towards Reverend answering, "No, not waiting on anyone. Just waiting."

"May I ask what it is you're waiting for?"

At the question, the man finally looked up into Reverend's

face. "You know, that's what's wrong with folks," he said looking back down at his foot. "Always gotta be waiting on something in particular. Sometimes..." and then he paused pulling a particularly large piece of dead skin off his heel. Reverend felt Ruth's sweet potato pie churning in the pit of his stomach. "Sometimes," the man continued, "you just gotta wait. You gotta wait for whatever and for however long."

Something about his explanation felt right to Reverend, so he moved on. "How many days you been here?"

"Don't remember. Memory's not what it used to be. Not long. Don't expect to be around much longer though." He looked up at the sky as if seeking confirmation. He lowered his right foot with a wince, rinsing it in a rain puddle on the stair and then started on the left.

"Well, I actually came out here looking for someone. The man that usually brings food out in the morning. Have you seen him?"

"Yup. But he's gone now."

Reverend felt a small sense of relief. "So you've seen him this morning? What time did he leave?"

"Wasn't out here this morning."

"But you just said you saw him."

"I did. But I didn't say when I saw him."

"Okay. So when? When did you see him, exactly? When did you see him leave?"

"Last night. It was late. Saw him walk out from behind that barn over there," he said pointing straight ahead, "and walked right by me and went around the side of the house. Never heard a motor. Never heard a door close. But I know he's gone."

"You sure he didn't come back this morning?"

"I've been back here since last night. Ain't heard a thing. Feet hurt too bad to move. Haven't had on a pair of shoes in a while." His face suddenly conveyed a look of confusion. "Who knew that walkin' could be so hard on feet? Ain't that what they made for?"

Although it seemed to be a genuine question, Reverend couldn't find the energy to offer an answer. "Well, sir, I'm truly sorry about your feet. I'm happy to pray for you if you wish."

"Naw, no need to waste your time on that. I'm good."

Reverend sighed a deep sigh and stepped up onto the side porch. He walked along the side of the house noticing empty containers and folded newspapers stacked neatly against the railing. And though the paint, what was left of it, peeled badly, the porch was swept clean. Now as he walked the side of the wrap-around porch there was a humming. He paused for a moment to find it. It was just in front of him so he looked past the eight-foot chokeberry bush and a sixty foot elm out to where the foot picking person said he had seen Gunther coming from. There at the side of the barn, laying against it, was one somebody with their legs stretched out humming at another somebody who lay in their arms, being rocked. Both, from where he could see, looked like two grown men. One in an overcoat wearing a hat and the other being rocked in a pair of jeans and a shirt. Reverend didn't understand what he was seeing. Grown men didn't let other grown men cradle them in their arms and rock them like a baby—humming at them.

The hairs on the back of his neck scratched against the inside of his collar and he made his way hurriedly toward the barn—toward the rocking man—to see who he was holding. He raced down the length of the side of the porch and to the back. The men were not visible from the back porch. He hurried along to the steps. He started down the six steps to the gravel drive, and as soon as his foot touched the ground the humming stopped. If someone, anyone, had asked him just at that moment what it was that was sitting heavy in the pit of his stomach, he would likely not have had an answer. But it sat and the weight of it made him lumber across the yard not noticing that the rain had started again.

By the time he reached the barn, there were no legs jutted out endlessly and no rocking man. There was not even an indication in the mud that something had been there. Reverend looked at the spot on the side of the barn and wondered at what dream state he had been in. Had they been there? Had he really seen them? Frantically, he twisted around once, then twice, looking out past the barn into the cornfield and then again towards the house, and then past the treeline. Finally, he walked to the door of the barn and looked in, air puffing from his flaring nostrils, rivulets of rain falling from the brim of his hat.

"Gunther! You in here? Gunther!"

All that returned to him was a hollow feeling. He stood there squinting in, deep and then deeper. The rain was getting heavier splashing mud up the back legs of his pants. Then finally he stepped in. And suddenly it was sixty years ago.

The barn, though uncompleted, was young compared to the rest of the property and was less for animals than it was for the homeless people. It wasn't original to the property, but had been built by many of them who came from nowhere and everywhere. There were two sway-back horses, so content to be just anywhere they wandered around the barn and in and out of their stalls with leisure. Hay scattered the floor and a cat and her kittens moved around without thought to hunger or harm. The sun sent halos of light and welcoming shadows amid the walls and the smell of the creatures was calming and interesting to a young man who had spent his time on cement sidewalks beside well-cared for lawns. There were shadows of him and Cooke everywhere. Echoes of giggles and boy talk blew on gentle air. And just as he made it to the center of the barn he looked straight ahead of him and he returned to the rain and fear. The back door of the barn stood wide open to the charred and hollowed out first barn, steam rising from the ground like the fire that destroyed it so long ago. The old barn like a horse with a broke leg refusing to lay down on its own even after all this time, waiting for someone to come and put it out of its misery, reminded Reverend of why he would never cross Cooke. Two homeless people had died in that fire. And the rumor amongst those that survived was that Cooke had been seen somewhere nearby. Someone said he had what looked like a gasoline can in one hand. Another said they saw him and yes, he was holding something, but couldn't be for certain what it was. Someone said they didn't know why anyone would want to accuse someone of such a heinous crime without some kind of substantial evidence. And someone else asked how could you believe otherwise with the kind of hatred he'd shown them? But they all agreed about other details of that day. About how Cooke never called for help. He didn't even go for a bucket of water. And when it was clear that whoever was in there didn't have a chance of getting out, he simply turned around and walked away.

It was during Carl's second trip to Becoming the tragedy happened. Momma O had gone to bed early that night. Something she rarely did. And something she never did again after that fire. But that was as much as he could remember. Initially he told Momma O he must have dozed off. When he woke up, he was at the creek but he couldn't remember how he'd gotten there. Momma O finally decided he must have been in shock from the screaming and all. He'd probably never seen anything like a barn being on fire in a fancy place like Chicago. But Carl had seen fires in Chicago. Big ones too. One day a whole tall building of apartments caught on fire and for a while, until his momma dragged him away, he watched people jumping out of windows and the firemen running in. He didn't remember being in shock then. It was the next morning that he and Cooke had fled Becoming, leaving everything he couldn't remember behind.

Reverend headed back to his car, slamming the door against the bursting sky. He hadn't notice that the person who had spent the night picking between their toes was gone. And just like the humming man, had left no mark.

FOUND

At seven fifty-five, Cooke gave up looking for Gunther at his home. At eight twenty-three, Reverend found him.

The finding happened at the end of his regular morning rounds at Mercy Hospital amid the rattling of pill carts and transporting beds. Prayers were done. People had been committed into the hands of a God who would go before them, guide the hands of their doctors and bring them out brand new from their various procedures. Reverend was one corridor and an automated door away from being gone from Mercy for the morning when his name was called.

"Reverend? If you got time this mornin', we have a man down in intensive care that we're havin' a bit of trouble puttin' a name to. You know a lot of people here in Becoming. Would you mind comin' down and taking a look?"

The nurse had a fresh pillowy black eye badly covered with make-up. It would probably have started conversation amongst people that didn't know her, but Reverend had known her for a long time, so he chose not to mention it as he followed her down the hall. In past conversations, he'd realized that she was perfectly accepting of her life, and who was he to mess with it?

She'd said she was finishing up back-to-back shifts, and would he mind going into room four alone while she signed out. But he was already looking past her into room four, so he didn't hear her when she said, "I'll be back in a minute or two." Nor did he hear her shoes squeaking away on the linoleum. Someone was suddenly beside him saying something about an accident that was probably on the news this morning. That the patient was driving a car that was going at least eighty miles an hour when it ran into Hank's Pizzeria. They said that several people were injured, some fatally. Had he seen it? They said the man in room four was now in a coma due to head trauma and that he had not regained consciousness since the accident. They had actually thought they had lost him at one point during the night, but he surprised them and started breathing again. Tests were still being run to make sure nothing else was causing the comatose state.

They said. They said. Later when he would leave, Reverend wouldn't remember who they were.

"Well? Do you know him?" they asked as he stood beside the bed.

Finally, after what seemed like a terrible stretch of time, Reverend said he did know the man. He had hired him years ago to work for him at the church. He was like a son to him.

So now that they had a name, they asked Reverend to pray for Mr. Ferguson because he certainly needed it. But Reverend was too stunned to pray immediately. And then when he teetered at the foot of the bed, they brought him a chair, and went back to their station when he promised to leave as soon as he caught his breath. So Reverend sat, elbows to knees in a green vinyl chair under the room's only window, leaning into the face of Gunther Ferguson.

ABOVE IT ALL

It had only been eight hours ago and eight blocks away from the drugstore when things went terribly wrong. The pain in his chest overtook him and his body went ramrod straight. Suddenly, behind the wheel of his well-cared for Chrysler, moving at forty miles per hour down Shepherd's Creek, on the slick, rain-soaked road, Gunther couldn't move. He wanted to stop the car. He tried to stop the car. But his body seemed a foreign thing, unable to respond at all to the simplest of commands. He attempted to scream to the God that Reverend assured him every Sunday was present at all times. But his tongue too had become leaden. So, he sent up a mental prayer, a quick one fashioned after words he'd heard from the pulpit on many a Sunday morning. Reverend Madison had often said that, "You don't have to pray a long drawn out prayer when you're in trouble. God knew you in the womb! He knows what you need before you even open your mouth!"

He found comfort in those words now, particularly since he couldn't move his lips. He simply thought, "Help me, Jesus!"

and waited for the car to stop. Reverend's grand exhortations rarely verified themselves in his life, but Gunther had great hopes that this one would be answered.

Traveling down the long end of the "T" in the road, he thought the evidence of God hearing him this time came in the way everything seemed to slow down to the pace of his "slow play" button on the DVD player—his breathing, the buildings that moved by him, and the people directly in front of him.

Straight ahead was Hank's Pizzeria. Even at this moment, he could not understand why anyone would want to buy pizza from a guy named Hank. A girl with too blue, blue eye shadow sat in the large front window poised to take a bite of Hank's pizza. Once the car's headlights hit the window, she turned towards it. The pizza went limp, her mouth went slack and her too blue, blue eye shadow got lost behind bulging eyes. Her companion sitting across from her turned towards the window. He jumped up from his chair gesturing wildly, his lips constantly moving. Gunther guessed he was screaming at Too Blue to move out of the way. He wanted to tell them they didn't have to move because any second now the car was going to stop. His foot would release the accelerator, his ramrod straight arms would relax, and the pain in his chest would go away. But as he sped closer, the boy jumped out of his chair and ran, tripping over chairs and shoving tables out of his way. Too Blue got stuck standing with her drink in one hand and her greasy slice of pizza in the other.

The car never did stop on its own. Another prayer gone unanswered. Instead, with a magnificent crash of metal and a shattering of glass it rammed right through Hank's brightly lit storefront, stopping just five feet shy of the counter. A splattering of blood and tomato sauce settled on the mangled hood.

Gunther's pain was now gone and it seemed Too Blue was also. But she resurfaced quickly. He watched as she slipped out from under the car through a haze of smoke. Up close he saw how beautiful she was. Ethereal-like. Her too blue eye shadow now unnoticed as she rose resplendently, moving higher and higher, gliding towards a light that was brighter than anything he had ever seen before. Once, she turned and motioned for him to follow, pausing briefly waiting for his response. But then she turned and was gone.

It was then he realized he too was free of his body. And not only free from it, but above it. Below him a fireman was using the Jaws of Life to try to extricate it from the Chrysler. A shard of glass with a green letter k on it protruded from the right eye and Hank's card reader was jammed in the side of the arm. The body was broken and covered in blood, and he was sure he was glad to be rid of it.

But he could see other things as well. Just in front of him he could see Hank stumbling around in his three room apartment pulling on his jeans as he kicked aside empty vodka pint bottles that littered the floor, while trying to sober up as he searched for his car keys. The night nurse at Mercy Hospital was informing staff of the incoming wounded as she covered a freshly blackened eye—a gift from her latest abuser. Too Blue's date was sitting in the back of an ambulance in shock trying to make sense of what had just happened. "I wanted to go get a burger," he said to the EMT. "But she just kept insisting that she wanted pizza—and not just any pizza. She lives two blocks from an Italian pizza parlor, for Christ's sake! But no! She had to have

Hank's tonight. If only we had stopped for gas like I wanted in the first place. Five minutes. Five minutes! That's all it would have been getting gas and we would have missed all this," he sobbed. "What will I tell her parents?"

But of course the Date didn't understand anymore than Gunther had moments ago. But for Gunther, there was clarity. Gunther understood everything. Every shadow, every whisper. Every thought and every action of everyone through time was now known. There was no present. There was no past. Time just was. Light as a feather and with a swoosh he turned looking behind him and could see Deacon Williams sitting on the front pew of Promisekeepers Church singing, "In that land of perfect day, when the mists have rolled away, we will understand it better by and by!" And his soul leapt in a chorus of jubilant "hallelujahs!" that were unencumbered by the body's hands and feet and full of unspeakable joy. He was home.

If only Too Blue's companion understood what had just happened, his joy for Too Blue's current condition would overwhelm his grief. If only Gunther could tell him it was the calling to this place that made her push to eat at Hank's. It was her time.

The faintest of sounds, like a tiny million pieces of broken crystal being poured out into a dry well, emanated from the light and it was deep and warm and called him to it. He hadn't noticed it as Too Blue had disappeared, but now he saw that the light was at the end of a long tunnel and he began to drift towards it.

"Gunther!"

Immediately he felt her spirit as his own. Her crossing over had not freed her as it had him. Her heaviness of grief disoriented him as he knew that it had no place here. She called his name again and he remembered her at the sink earlier breathing on the nape of his neck. She had been preparing him then. It wasn't his time like it had been for Too Blue. She was the one that had called him here. Everything seemed to stop. And once again, as it had been for most of the time in his body, it was just him and her.

There was no speaking here, no mouths making noises, no lips that were always moving—always moving. Thoughts were simply perceived. And her thoughts thundered against his spirit.

"You haven't kept your promise, son!"

He watched her murky spirit as it jerked and sputtered. It had been a long time since those days of hoping his mother would find his daddy and bring him home. Not so much because he wanted it, but he thought if she could find him, she wouldn't get lost behind her eyes any more. Gunther turned back to his mother reassuring her that his father would be on his way. Certainly soon, he thought, if he knew both of them were there waiting on him and particularly after all of his years of work. But it didn't seem to bring her any comfort. There was no sense of reassurance.

"You made a promise to me, son. A promise. And I'm holdin' you to it. Now, go back! Bring him to me!"

THE RAT

There were other residents of Becoming, the ones of the four legged sort, who were finding their own challenges in the uncompromising weather pattern. A particular black rat who had lived in the sewers for the entirety of its thirteen month life had been paddling through the rising waters for two days. As luck would have it, its watery journey took it into a drain where with great effort it was able to push through the crack of an ill-placed drain cover and climb out onto dry land. At the edge of the drain hole it shivered in its new surroundings until the promise of a fresh meal wafted by in a thin breeze causing it to rise up on its haunches. Its nose twitched, flinging droplets of water from its whiskers. A brief study of the room and it clicked across the floor to a neatly stacked pile of newspapers. The stack of papers ended at a shelving unit and it made its way across the top shelf and then flung itself onto the hood of a truck. Just then, its meal emitted a hissing sound which may have given it pause had it not been so hungry, but it was focused on its lunch. It made its way down the tarp that lay across the back of the truck just as a hand slid out from underneath it. Perfect timing. It sniffed for what would be the best place to start and then it began to nibble at one of the fingers. It feasted for quite a long time taking the flesh and bone just past the second knuckle of the hand. A bit of dried blood and slivers of bone dusted the truck floor. When it had its fill, it curled itself up on the tarp and closed its eyes. Having eaten so thoroughly it did not flinch a muscle when the heavy gold insignia ring slid off what was left of the finger and fell to the floor, bounced once and then rolled gently past the floor drain, coming to rest just at the corner of the garage door.

STANDING IN THE RAIN

Breakfast was late. The early morning news show had already been on for more than forty minutes and breakfast still had not been served. But they waited. Throwaway people waiting for throwaway food, dripping under the "Enter Here" sign of the Promisekeepers Church.

Standing in a stupor at the front of the line was Reverend. Since leaving Gunther in Mercy's intensive care, he had not uttered a word. Not to the pillowy-eyed nurse as he left the floor, or to the cataract patient who sat in a wheelchair with discharge papers in hand calling out to him, "Reverend, it was your prayer that made the difference. Surgery went well and I'm seeing better already!" It wasn't until his name was called that he even realized he was not alone. And then, the calling so startled him that his keys which were poised to unlock the side door went flying from his hands and landed in a fissure that was forming between the building and the landing.

"You okay, Reverend?"

He looked up at the long line of brown faces. Most of them

were regulars, except for the two or three whose first time was today. Tomorrow they would be regulars too. A handful could say they were natives of Becoming. The others had wandered into town from some forgotten place and somehow never left, content to sleep in unoccupied spaces and eat where food was offered. Life's circumstances had stolen away the promise of hardworking men and woman. And for some, stolen away their minds.

"Reverend!" Evaline stamped her foot down hard, her large dimpled thigh jiggling underneath a threadbare floral dress. "Look at this damn cheap thread. Damn cheap," she muttered. She held empty fingers up for Reverend to see. "How do they expect me to get all these beads on these dresses in time if I have to stop every five minutes to rethread this damn needle!"

Evaline and Gail had been coming to the church for more than six weeks. In all that time, Reverend had barely given them more than a polite nod. Gail had told him the story of how they had come to be homeless, laid off from a factory job, no money for rent or food and kicked out of their car. Too young for social security and too old to start a new career. He hadn't paid much attention to the details because that was someone else's job.

"You see this cheap thread, Gail?" She thrust her empty fingers into the face of the woman standing by her side. "You see how thin it is? Always trying to save a buck. First they switch to these cheap beads that peel and crack like boiled eggs, and now this cheap thread. Watch—next week they're gonna give us colored markers and have us draw 'em on." Evaline roared. "That's pretty funny, ain't it Reverend? Huh? Gail? That's pretty funny, ain't it?"

"Yes, Evaline. That's pretty funny," answered Gail whose glance at Reverend suggested she would bear the shame of Evaline's insanity if Evaline couldn't bear it on her own.

Evaline snickered into her stained jacket sleeve and then quickly got back to her task. "Even if I get the beads on, they're not gonna stay on with this cheap thread. Do you see it, Gail? Do you see it?"

"Yes, Evaline, I see it."

With her eyes squinted into tiny slits and her lips pursed wet and tight, Evaline held her hands high in the air catching the light just so before trying to shove the thread that wasn't really there through the eye of the needle that wasn't really there. Finally, after a few stabs, it seemed to be in. And with a twist of the wrist, a magical knot was formed, and she was back to work. Slowly at first, and then working her way up to a steady rhythm, rocking back and forth on the balls of her feet. Forward, pick up a bead. Backwards, stick it on the end of the needle. Forward, push the needle down through the fabric. Backwards, pull the needle back up.

"Okay, now Evaline, time to put that away." Gail laid a hand on Evaline's arm. "They'll be letting us in for breakfast soon, and you wouldn't want to get that beautiful gown dirty." Gail smiled a crooked smile at Reverend while Evaline muttered and folded the dress, ending with putting the needle into the pincushion. Once she settled down, Gail gently laid her hand atop her friends' arm.

"Sumpin's wrong, Reverend!" Somewhere in midline, a man's face jutted out.

"What are you talking about now, Jerry Miller? You don't

know anything of the sort," Gail said with a leave me alone sort of tone. "Sorry, Reverend," she said, "he's just impatient. I done told him you can't be impatient when people are being as good to you as y'all are to us."

The stocky bald man, wearing a blue and orange plaid jacket leaned around the line. He shuffled his feet in a pair of strapped on makeshift shoes. "I ain't being impatient!" he said adamantly. "The truck ain't here. Gunther's truck is always here. And the doors are still locked. It's almost nine o'clock, and them doors are still locked. And where's George? You know George, don'cha Reverend?" His eyes widening. "He's the one wears them dirty, ole red sneakers. He don't miss any free meals."

Reverend looked down the line wondering if he would know George if he saw him.

Gail responded. "You ol' man. Just cause the truck ain't here don't mean a thing. Everybody's late sometime. Well, this is Gunther's time to be late, ain't it, Reverend? And as far as George is concerned, he was crabbin' about not feeling well yesterday. Maybe he just decided to sleep in this mornin'. You know—have the maid wake him up late." Gail chuckled. "And anyway, how do you know what time it is? You ain't never owned a watch in all the weeks I've known ya."

"Don't need a watch to know what time it is," Jerry retorted. "And don't have to have a college degree to know something's wrong. Something's wrong, I tell ya. Something just ain't right!" He disappeared back into the line.

The seed of doubt Jerry planted bore fruit with Gail. "Y'all is gonna feed us this morning, aren't y'all? I mean, I do smell something in there." Her eyes rolled toward the door and then back to Reverend.

"Now you all just settle down." Reverend unlocked the door with his retrieved keys and pulled it open. "We just had a little delay this morning, but I'm sure they're almost ready to let you all in. I appreciate you all being so patient," he said as he slipped through the door and pushed it closed.

Inside, Julia was standing in the bathroom for the fourth time since Cooke and Reverend's earlier departure. Her four trips might have gone unnoticed had she not recruited Carlita away from her ammonia shissing bottle to keep an eye on things in the kitchen every time. Each time she called Carlita over, Carlita put a number to it. "This is the second time, now. Oh, so now you have to go a third time? What is this? You sick or somethin'?"

A while ago, Carlita had come banging on the bathroom door, insisting that Julia hurry and return to the kitchen because Cooke was back and she didn't want to be in there alone with him. And besides, she really didn't know what she was doing. Her job was setting the tables and she was done with that. The intensity of Carlita's banging had so scared Julia that the toothpick she had been jabbing into the soft flesh of her inner thigh as she stood against the door of the stall broke and she was now trying to decide if she was going to leave it in or try to fish it out.

The past twelve hours or so had been the same but different and she wondered if Gunther's absence had to do with something she'd done.

With trembling fingers, she pushed on the embedded toothpick, driving it deeper into her flesh. And without expression squeezed at it leaving nail prints. Rhythmically, she pushed and squeezed and pushed and squeezed until finally small tiny droplets of blood spattered her leg. She blew her breath through her parted lips. Suddenly, Reverend's voice pierced her haze and she hurriedly grabbed a piece of tissue and dabbed at the blood. She shoved down her dress and went back into the hall.

Carlita was calling out to Reverend through the kitchen pass through window. "What did you say, Reverend? Did you find Gunther? Hold on a minute." She reappeared at the kitchen door. "Now what was that?" she asked. "Is Gunther here with the truck?"

"Go b-b-back to peeling them potatoes, girl, I got this." Cooke squeezed past her through the doorway wiping his hands on his apron. Julia slid down into a nearby chair to listen.

"How come the doors are still closed?" Reverend demanded.

"Things been a little disrupted since we left this morning. Still ain't seen hide nor hair of Gunther. Wasn't at his house neither." He looked over Reverend's shoulder at her. "And I can't seem to keep this one in the kitchen this morning. Woman, would you open them doors up and get those folks in out the rain?" Julia looked over at the door and then back at Reverend's left hand. He was holding Gunther's keys. No good would come of him holding Gunther's keys.

"Well, no—wait a minute, Ms. Julia. I got some news," said Reverend. It wasn't that he'd said he had news that made the room go still. It was the way in which he said it, like he knew the gates of hell had broken loose. He went on to explain what he knew about Gunther. When he was finished the two men stood quietly for a moment. She looked up at Cooke who looked like Reverend had just made up a story. Like none of what he had just said was true.

"He's in a coma?" Cooke's normal scowl was replaced by something different. Something softer.

Reverend simply answered with a nod as the corners of his mouth twitched. "I've got to get over to Gunther's house. They're going to need a family member who can make decisions." Reverend's eyes locked with Cooke's. "Fortunately, they also found his keys," he said holding them up. "I hope to be able to find a personal phone book. If he has any living relatives, I would hope they would be in there."

"Kitty Carlisle." The name came so quickly and so easily even Julia couldn't believe she'd said it.

"Beg pardon, Sister Julia?"

"His aunt's name. Um, um, I've heard him speak of her before. Kitty Carlisle. She doesn't live far from here, I think, but I don't know where."

"Thank you, sis," replied Reverend, his voice full of questions. "I'm sure that's gonna help me considerably. Now, listen," he said addressing the whole room, "I've got a couple of things that I have to attend to first in my office. But then I'll head straight over there. I'm certain to be gone a while. But I want things to go on as usual as much as possible. Get what you have of breakfast out to the warmers and get those people out of the rain."

With one more glance at Cooke, Reverend disappeared down the hallway. For a while the stunned workers didn't move. And then Cooke called out.

"What did Reverend just say?" Still no one moved. "Get going! Now!" And as the room again fluttered with activity, Julia grabbed her purse and headed out the back door.

THE FIRST TIME

He could feel her eyes on him dredging his skull for gold as he stood on Gunther's doorstep. Reverend worked quickly to unlock the front door, knowing that today the nuggets lay just below the surface—easy pickings for a woman like Hattie Mae.

He had only been face to face with her once. On a particularly blustery day seven years ago, he'd looked up after blessing the morning's offering to find her crooked silhouette hovering in the doorway of his church. At the end of the service he ignored the usual outstretched hands and raced down the aisle to greet her. After a brief exchange of cordialities, he asked her what had brought her there. Her reply was simple.

"Just checkin', Reverend. Just checkin'." When she spoke, her head bobbed up and down on a thin, veined neck.

The ring of keys that had been pressed into his hand by somebody at the hospital were cumbersome and he wondered at their extravagance in Gunther's very pedestrian life. It took some time of stabbing at the lock with the wrong keys while dodging Hattie Mae's eyes before the right key slid in.

He had never been in Gunther's house before. So the "honey, I'm home" feeling that swept over him as he entered the living room was unnerving. The feeling crawled up his spine causing him to tighten his coat belt and tug at his tie. Yet there was a sense that before he had entered the room it was filled with people. And when the key had turned, they had slipped behind the doors and the furniture—waiting, holding their breath. He looked around the room for shadows in the stormy light of the morning. It was warm and it was quiet. He wouldn't stay long.

The past had been well-preserved here—all clean and crisp and covered in plastic. Directly across from him on the wall was Jesus kneeling at a rock with hands folded in front of him, gazing up into a light from above. It seemed everyone he knew growing up had that painting in their living room. On both sides and above the painting hung crosses. It wasn't a big house and Reverend felt he filled it just standing at the door. The furnishings were sparse—a sofa, two chairs and a coffee table. Reverend shook rain droplets from his overcoat and the beginning of a chill from underneath it and then headed towards a hallway to his left.

There were three closed doors to look behind. The first room, still as death, was dressed with a pink chenille bed cover. There were no paintings or hangings on the striped wallpapered wall. And the dresser tops were as bare as the floor with the exception of one brush and one handheld mirror. Reverend didn't feel compelled to move any farther into the room than the doorway. And even though he knew he was alone, he still called out, "Huh?" and waited for a moment before closing the door behind him.

The next room was the bathroom, and it glistened with early 1900s black and white tiles. A single blue and white striped toothbrush hung in the holder on the wall.

On the way to the third room Reverend caught a glimpse of some photographs that lined the wall. In that brief glance something seemed familiar—felt familiar, but he was too distracted by his desire to find Gunther's phone book and leave the house to stop. Then, in the stillness, he heard a thump—and then another. He turned towards the living room and waited, his back to the last door.

A few seconds later, he attributed the noise to the furnace again kicking on or off and continued. On the way back down the hall he would stop at the thermostat and shut it down. There was no need to keep the furnace going in an empty house.

There was another thump. It was definitely coming from beneath him. He pulled himself away from his wondering and turned the handle on the last door. He wanted to be out of there.

It was obvious this room was Gunther's. The bed faced the door and at the foot was a pair of leather slippers. Neatly folded across the bottom of the bed was a man's summer robe. The room was as bare as the front bedroom with the exception of a lamp on the right nightstand and a pitcher of water and a cup on a tray. Reverend pushed open the door and looked around the room. He pulled the door back to him just a bit and looked behind it. To his left was the closet. He took off his hat and moved hesitantly towards it. He laid his hand on the glass knob and cocked his head to the side listening. Twice he glanced over his shoulder with expectation. Another thump and he moved to the right side of the bed, sitting on its edge.

He was relieved upon opening the drawer on the bedside table to find two small books tucked away in a corner alongside two neatly placed, sharpened pencils.

He stuck his hat crookedly back on his head and began to leaf through the first book. There were dates and a name. Not different names for each entry, but one name. Father Ferguson. And each Father Ferguson had a number next to it. Some pages only had one entry and some pages had none. Reverend did not know why, but the small seemingly insignificant book made him feel even more uncomfortable.

"Thump!" Reverend slammed the book closed, almost dropping both onto the floor. He quickly switched them and began leafing through the second one. Though sparse, it held regular phone entries. "Thump!" Initially his thought was to find the address book, make the call to Gunther's aunt, and leave the house. But he didn't like being here. So he quickly stuffed the books into his inside coat pocket and ventured back out into the hallway. But then he remembered the wallet. The hospital had not been able to identify Gunther because he didn't have a wallet on him. Reverend had been charged with finding it not only for official identification, but also to see if there was an insurance card in it. Reluctantly, he stepped back into the bedroom. And from there to the kitchen. He searched every reasonable place a man might forget his wallet. The dresser. The bathroom counter. The living room table. The kitchen counter. It was nowhere to be found. He deduced it must have been thrown from the car at the accident site.

He heard the noise again, but this time it was a little clearer as he was standing rather close to the door in the kitchen behind which it came. He assumed the door led down to the basement. He went over to it and jiggled the knob. It was locked. He almost felt relieved. Then he remembered the keys in his pocket and pulled them out. Such a lot of keys, at least fifteen.

"You know, Lord," he said aloud, "this would be a good time to do your thing and take care of whatever is making—." Suddenly on the seventh key, Reverend realized the noise had stopped. And never one to miss an opportunity, Reverend stuck the keys back in his pocket and took off for the front door.

HOVERING—
AND HE REMEMBERED

There was no way he was getting back in there. It was broken beyond good repair. The emergency surgery had stopped some bleeding, but for all of the tubes and wires connected to it, the body would never be the same. And even if by some Godly miracle, a conclusion was reached that it could return to normal, there had been too many hands on it now. In the last few hours more hands had been on it than had ever been when he had possessed it. Then, he might have welcomed some of the touching. It seemed ironic that the feeling of being alive came not when in the body, but after having left it. Nonetheless, the hands that drew blood, catheterized, lifted and cut at the body now owned it to do as they pleased. He didn't want it anymore even though his mother had shoved him and insisted that he return to it. But now, here in this space, he realized the choice was his to make. So without any need to participate in the doings below, he hovered.

Up above the bed in a corner of the room, as he watched the flurry of activity going on below him, he realized he was becoming more and more aware that there was no sense of time as he had known it in the body. He was before birth, he was a child, he was a man, he was eternal, he was all of it together all at once. And he was able to see the entirety of the life of Gunther Ferguson playing in front of him as on a movie screen.

Pushed by a shadow that slinked across the room like some dark outback creature hunting its prey, the day ran into a corner of the ceiling and disappeared, taking with it all of its butterfly-filled emotions. Lying in the middle of his mother's well-starched, well-pressed bed, Gunther imagined he had helped push it along as he drummed his fingertips one against the other high up above himself with each new rendition of the Itsy Bitsy Spider.

He was certain that the light knew that when he sang his song and bantered with the chittering crickets, it was time for the night to come save him and wrap him up in its safe quietness. Knew it was time for him to stop being lost in his six-year-oldness and find courage in being her other man, as she called him—had called him for as long as he could remember. The delight of knowing he was so well thought of was always enough to keep him steadfast in his mission to stay there in the middle of his mother's bed until she returned. Until she came back to lay beside him, caressing the top of his head and tenderly running her hand down the side of his arm and loving him into a deep sleep.

Tonight she was taking a little longer. He could tell by the stillness in the air. Most of the time when she returned, the rest of the world had not yet quieted down. He could usually hear the radio from down the way, and every now and then a trickle of laughter would float in through the curtains. And he would sing in a whisper in the dark to the two teenagers he knew were responsible for his toes dancing under the sheets, "You're gonna be in trouble, you're gonna be in trouble." He had also noticed there had not been a car horn for a while blaring things like, "I'll see you when I get back," or "I'm home—is dinner ready yet?" He remembered once she had come back even later than this time, but that had been so long ago, the longer he thought about it, the more uncertain he was that it had really happened.

His small brown eyes began to grow heavy and he changed his game to raising and lowering his eyelids with his fingers. Holding them open until he could not stand the burning any longer. It worked for a short time, but soon his fingers began to slip away from his face, and his breathing became a bit more even. The cramping pains in his stomach that always came with the sunrise eased, and the tenseness that was a part of who he was seemed less a part of him. But then she came. Her way was to always spend time outside and downstairs first before she finally would come to bed. Once he knew she was back, it was easy to stay awake.

"Where you been? I almost got scared." His mind was filled with the sounds he had heard coming from outside the window and below him in the basement as he had waited for her to come to bed. The opening and shutting of the garage door, the clinking together of the yard tools, and the moaning and banging of the water pipes. Familiar sounds in a familiar sequence. Gunther turned on his side to face her and wrapped his arm around her neck, studying her face.

"Out lookin' for your daddy, baby. Just trying' to find your

daddy," she said, as she pulled the covers up over her hips.

"Did you find him this time?" Her eyes went empty like they sometimes did, and he rubbed her cheek. "Momma? You in there?" He waited for an answer, and when one didn't come, he kept talking so he wouldn't lose her. "He's awfully hard to find, ain't he? Where you think he's at, Momma? You think he's still somewhere here in Becoming, or somewhere else?"

She finally returned to him. "Somewhere between here and somewhere else I suppose." She sighed and slipped a hand under her cheek, sinking deeper into her pillow.

"You think he's still living in the streets or do you think someone let him come stay with 'em?"

"I don't know, baby. I just don't know."

"He's kinda like Whiskers, ain't he, Momma?"

She seemed a bit more interested now. "Whiskers?"

"Yeah, the catfish Mr. Leon almost caught. He kept saying, 'I almost got him, I almost got him.' But I never seen him." He thought he saw the flicker of a smile in her eyes.

"Saw him."

"Saw him what?"

"No—you never saw him, not seen him."

Gunther let his arm slip from her neck. "I wish you wouldn't teach me about good English when I'm talkin'. I get all mixed-up."

His mother turned and snapped off the bedside lamp behind her.

"Did you plant more flowers, Momma?"

"Yes, baby, I planted more flowers," she answered as she nestled back down into the pillow.

"How come you always plant flowers in the dark, Momma? How come?" Once again he began to play with his fingers and turned his head slightly so he could hear her better.

"I already told you a hundred times, Gunther. I'm what you call fair-skinned, baby. Fair-skinned people like me don't need to be out in the sun gettin' sunburned."

"What kind of flower did you plant this time, Momma."

"Lilacs. I love the way lilacs smell."

"I know why you planted lilacs, Momma."

"Why, baby? Why did Momma plant lilacs?"

"Cause they smell so good, maybe Daddy will smell them and come home."

She smiled in the dark at him and stroked his head. "And until my big man comes home?"

"Your little man will be all the man you need," he said content that he would always be there for her on the nights after she planted the flowers.

THE WOMAN WITH THE GOLD SHOES

"Look at her, Gail! Just look at her standing over there. She's been standing there for an awful long time. What's she doing? Waiting for the ark to pull up?" Evaline squealed and then squinted with all seriousness.

During the warm weather months after breakfast, the hall would be emptied of diners so that the kitchen crew could clean and prepare for the mid-day meal. But during the winter or when the weather was particularly poor as had been for the last couple of days, the diners were allowed to remain as long as they didn't cause too much confusion. So the breakfast crowd was now the "waiting for lunch" crowd, and Evaline sat next to Gail guarding her place. Jerry Miller sat just across the table from them reading a section of the parceled out morning paper. Evaline was looking past Jerry through the crack of the propped door. Just through the crack on the other side of the street stood a woman who looked to Evaline to be about forty, standing lop-sided with one gold-flecked shoe on and one shoe off. Evaline had tilted her head just enough to straighten the woman up in her view.

"I bet you she's a spy," Evaline whispered. "I bet the company sent her down here to spy on us! To see if we're doing what we're supposed to be doing. But I done told them about this dress I'm working on. How am I supposed to do what I'm supposed to be doing if they don't send me the stuff I need? Look at this stuff, Gail! Look at this stuff they're trying to get me to use to make these dresses. I can't get these dresses done in time with this stuff!"

"Evaline, honey, I really don't think she's a spy. Why would she be standing out there in the rain?" Gail didn't really expect an answer—at least not one that made sense. It was just nice having a conversation with someone. People who had their own kitchens and made their own breakfasts never looked at them, let alone talked to them. Evaline's eyebrow raised and she stopped cold, squinting and looking out the door at the girl.

"Now you know, Gail, I'm not the kind who would argue with you…,"—a crooked grin slid up one side of Gail's face as she remembered the last five or six times just this morning that Evaline had disagreed with her—"but," she continued, "I'm pretty sure she is a spy. Why else would she be standing over there in them gold shoes?"

Jerry glanced up from his paper and took a quick look across the street. Looking back down at his paper he said, "She don't look like no spy to me. Spies try to go unnoticed. How you gonna go unnoticed with them shoes?" He glanced up again. "It is odd however that she been standin' there so long, and she don't look like she's homeless today. But now tomorrow… that's another day." Jerry went back to his paper. For a moment it was quiet and then he grunted. "They at it again!" Gail leaned towards the paper looking to see what he was reading.

"At what?"

"Them politicians up there need to mind their own business. They tryin' to figure out where to dump us next. Says here that the mayor is going to make staying out at the farm illegal. Gonna start arresting folks for vagrancy. Now why they got to come out there meddlin'? We way out there out of the way and they meddlin'. If the folks here don't mind and Gunther don't mind feedin' us, why they got to be bothered?"

Gail looked up from the paper, her eyes starting to glaze over. She wondered when in life it had been decided that she would be one of them. The homeless. Was it in her mother's womb? Or the first time she got an answer wrong in kindergarten? Or was it when she decided college was not affordable? When was it?

"Says here," continued Jerry, "that Mayor Brody is bringing it up for a vote in a couple of days. And you know," he said looking up from the paper and relaxing his eyes, "once it comes up for a vote, they've already done decided. I remember the last place I settled. It was a city down by the Ohio River. There was a small camp of us living under a bridge. Wasn't hurtin' nobody. Couldn't even see us unless you come looking for us. Some kind folks came by one Christmas and gave out some tents. Don't you know it wasn't two weeks and they sent the police to come tear 'em down. They confiscated the tents and told us if we didn't move on, we'd end up in jail. Now what kind've stuff is that? Why they got to treat us so poorly all the time? Don't we matter to nobody?"

Gail was tired. Tired of trying to find a place to live and a place to die. And even now tired of Evaline's chattering.

"I need better thread, I need better thread!" Evaline gently rocked back and forth on her seat, a look of confusion and sadness on her face. Gail watched Evaline for a moment and then suddenly she was there. No longer a figure in the door slit, the gold shoe holding woman was standing in front of Gail. Evaline gasped.

"Can you help me?" She looked much younger up close. Twenty-five or thirty. "I'm looking for a man by the name of Kevin Kelley. He left out yesterday on his way here to this church and I haven't seen him since. He's a thin dark-skinned man. Six one or so. Had on a bright yellow suit and a bowler hat with a feather in it. Good hair. Seen him?"

A CUT AND LOSES

"Dammit!"

"Mr. Cooke, what happened? Are you okay?" Carlita raced over to the counter where Cooke had been chopping herbs for the dinner soup. After a morning in the bathroom, Julia had disappeared and Carlita had reluctantly taken her place. She looked down and saw a stream of blood running into the herbs. "Oh, my goodness! Here, let me help…"

"Girl, stop fussing. It's nothin'," Cooke responded shoving her hand away. He went to the sink and held his finger under the water. Blood filled the sink. Carlita handed him a dishtowel.

"I think you're going to need stitches, Mr. Cooke. We need to get you to the emergency room."

"I ain't going to no emergency room!" snapped Cooke.

"But, Mr. Cooke…"

"No, I said!" Cooke wrapped the towel around his finger and pressed hard. The bleeding was relentless.

"Well, then, come up to the nurses office and let me wrap it."

"I'm not a baby. I can manage this myself."

"If you don't get it taken care of, it could get infected and you could end up having to get a tetanus shot. Do you want to have to get a series of shots?"

As much as Cooke hated fussin' over, he hated shots more. So after a few more terse words he agreed to go with Carlita to the nurse's room. As he walked through the lobby, he caught a side glimpse of the woman whose unexpected appearance and words had caused his slip of the knife. He hoped she would be gone when he returned.

The nurse's room was really just a corner of the church office that was signaled by the defibrillator that hung on the wall. Below it on the floor was a well-stocked first aid kit and Carlita was able to find everything she needed in it. But what she was unable to do was stop the bleeding.

"You're gonna have to go to a hospital, Mr. Cooke," she said with a defeated sigh.

"I already told you, I ain't goin'! And even if I have to, I'll be the one to make the decision when, where or how. It wouldn't be bleedin' so bad if you would just leave it alone."

"That's nonsense, Mr. Cooke. I've already tried to wrap it three times. The tip of your finger is almost hanging off." She returned the supplies to the nurse's kit. "That's the best I can do for you. I hope you don't wait too long and lose too much blood. You could get woozy and pass out. Then we'll have to call 911, and I'll be stuck in that kitchen by myself tryin' to make your greens. Is that what you want?"

Cooke looked down at his finger with a cocked eyebrow. He hadn't thought about how losing blood might cause him to pass out. He wondered if Carlita was just messing with him.

Carlita, knowing she had struck a nerve, turned her back on him and smiled as she set the first aid kit back up against the wall. "I'm going back to the kitchen, Mr. Cooke. You decide what you're gonna do."

"You just go cut up the rest of those tomatoes real fine and get 'em cooking for the soup."

"Yessir. Gottcha." Carlita slammed the door shut behind her.

Cooke listened until he could no longer hear any noise from the hallway and then slid down from the table. "Well, now, Brother Kelley. This is 'bout the best opportunity I'll have to check on you," he whispered into the air. "Guess I better get to it." He cracked open the door and peeked out. Carlita was nowhere to be seen. He grabbed a towel from the metal table beside the door and wrapped his hand in it as he stepped out into the hallway. Promisekeepers was a large church. This wing consisted mostly of unmanned offices, a choir room, and a rehearsal hall. Fortunately for him, rarely was there anyone in this wing of the church on any day other than Sunday. He headed down the hall in the opposite direction of where Carlita had gone. At the end of this hall were five steps that led down to an outside door. The door let out onto a landing. Connected to the main facility was an abandoned daycare center. Underneath the landing was a storage area. The daycare had kept their garbage cans there. The center had been closed for three years now and the building committee of the church continued to suggest removing the cans, but no one had. It seemed to Cooke there had been more cans last night, but it was dark and he had been otherwise occupied. At the bottom of the landing he turned and looked around him making certain no one had gotten lost and rambled into the area. It was chilly out and he had to stifle a couple of sneezes in the side of the towel.

He had already had one cup of herbal tea since having come back from Gunther's, the same kind he had offered Kevin Kelley last night when they reunited. Only he didn't have the same allergy to tea that Kevin Kelley had. He was sure it would be in his best interest to have another cup when he got back to the kitchen.

Cooke pulled aside two strategically placed dented cans to reveal the door that at one time had been painted a straw color to match the color of the church's brick. But having weathered through the years, only a few specks of paint here and there remained. The door itself had been made of five slats of wood nailed together. At one time straight and level, the slats were now buckled and ratty. Yesterday when Cooke had shut the door forcing the bottom corner across the concrete ground, he recalled seeing a corner of Kevin Kelley's coat sticking out from under the door. It had been a hard process pulling the dead weight down the hallway and down the steps to the storage bin, and by the time Cooke had gotten him in and started shutting the door, he wasn't about to open it back up for such a small detail. So he was just careful the cans hid it before he left. But it wasn't there now. Out in the cold of the wet day, beads of sweat began to form on the otherwise cool head of Cooke. "Ain't no way anyone could have found you under here," he mumbled. "Ain't no way. But I imagine," he continued as a furrow grew across his brow, "that rats could have." He wasn't at all happy about the prospect of finding a rat in that hole with Kelley. And him out in the open with nothing to defend himself. By the time he began tugging on the rusty handle of the door, he was positive that some type of vermin or animal had chewed away the piece of material and was now inside chewing away at Kelley's rigid body. There was nowhere to run to even if he could still run, so Cooke positioned himself behind the door in case anything needed to escape. The edge of the door again grated against the concrete pathway as it had the night before when he had opened it for the first time. Only this time it seemed louder. Finally with one good hard jerk, it flew open against him and Cooke had to turn his head to keep the door from hitting him in the face. He leaned in looking into the small hole. Kevin Kelley was gone and all that was left was a great gaping black storage facility.

DEAD AND GONE

Kelley was dead when he put him in the storage space less than twenty-four hours ago. So where was the body?

Cooke took the two steps up onto the cracked asphalt parking lot and in the pouring rain stood still as a sleeping newborn. There was nothing like a predicament to calm his spirit. Ever so slowly he scanned the surrounding area—the lot, the fence that surrounded it and a few feet beyond—looking for some indication of what could have happened. If someone had found Kelley, surely there would have been some kind of commotion—police, a call to the Reverend, news reporters. But there hadn't been. So maybe Kelley really hadn't been dead. Cooke had heard of people who seemed dead, buried even, but suddenly began breathing again. Had that been the case? He went back to the storage unit door and looked in one more time as if he could have missed a grown man in such a small space. He slammed the door shut and started back inside but then abruptly stopped. He looked behind him. Last night he had pulled two of four garbage cans in front of the storage door.

Two were gone. He went back out into the rain and looked down the side of the church. The cans were nowhere to be seen. Suddenly he was aware of the throbbing pain beneath the blood soaked gauze around his hand. He was going to have to go to the hospital. But it would give him an opportunity to check on Gunther. He headed back to his apartment to get his coat leaving streaks of blood on the door frame.

He half expected another surprise appearance from Kelley as had been the case the night before. As he walked across the living room floor, he stopped occasionally thinking about all that had transpired between him and the witness.

It was late when he had finally finished up in the kitchen. Nine-thirty in the evening. The dinner crowd had left on time—six thirty or so, but it was inventory night. Inventory happened once every two months, just in time for the budget committee meetings and always the night before garbage pickup. Julia had stayed late to help as she always did. Earlier there had been a call from a nearby farm. A grocer a few miles away had forgotten to pick up his eggs and the farmer didn't want them to go to waste. So Cooke called Gunther who had long been gone but agreed to make the pickup. In the meantime, he and Julia counted cans of beans and paper plates, dumping expired foods and old foil pans. Just about the time the last garbage bag was set near the door and the last fork had been counted, Gunther returned with the eggs. A tired Cooke left Julia and Gunther to close up.

In the space he'd been allowed to use in the church basement, Cooke had partitioned it so he had a small sitting room, bedroom and small makeshift kitchen. He had also converted some fixings for a laundry area into a bathroom. No tub, just a shower.

For weeks he had been waking up at three and four in the morning and not getting back to sleep. The constant rain had not only brought a sense of foreboding, but it flared his arthritis. He was looking forward to a hot shower and a warm bed.

Just on the other side of a dried wicker tri-panel that separated his living domain from the rest of the basement was a bookcase that divided his kitchen from his living room. As always, he started emptying his pockets of keys and loose change. There were only two lights in this room. One was a tall, narrow brass lamp constructed from an old fountain topped with a bright yellow shade he'd found trashing one night. The other was a floor lamp that hung over his reading chair. Both were on the opposite side of the room—the only side that had electrical outlets. But even when he came home as late as it was, it didn't bother him that he had to walk around in the dark for a while before he had access to a light because he knew his home so well. In fact, some nights he never turned them on at all. He pulled his sweater over his head and tossed it across the room in the general area of his dirty clothes pile. And it was then when it landed that he got the feeling something was off. Not given to panic, he took his time and stood rubbing the back of his neck, casually glancing around the room as his eyes adjusted to the dark. Suddenly the floor light clicked on.

"Been a long time, Cooke," he'd said. Kevin Kelley sat back in Cooke's salvaged black leather recliner. His brown feathered bowler resting on his crossed leg.

"Reverend told me you were in town."

"I thought you'd be glad to see me."

Cooke dropped his head and ran a thumb across his right eyebrow. "I might've been, had this been under different circumstances."

"Different how?"

"Like I said, Reverend told me you were in town." Cooke looked up and glared across the room.

Kelley chuckled. "How long you been calling him Reverend?"

The men took a moment away from the niceties to take a good look at one another, summing each other up. They had known each other for more than forty years. When Reverend and Cooke had first moved to Detroit, they shared an apartment with the native Detrotian. He had helped finance the restaurant that Reverend and Cooke had gone there to open. And up until Reverend and Cooke had moved back to Becoming, they had been almost constant companions.

"What brings you here?"

"I thought you just said you talked to Carl?"

Cooke grinned slightly. He rubbed his chin and then stuck his hands in his pocket. "Hmm, I did, didn't I? But I really meant here—in my home." Cooke rounded the overturned orange crate he called an end table and sat down on the sofa. He pulled his shoes off and laid a tired foot up on the edge of another orange crate he called a coffee table. "What's going on with you, Kelley? Reverend said something about you trying to blackmail him." Cooke sat close enough now to smell the same poor smell that the others had who came with their hands out to the church.

Kelley chuckled. "Ah, man, don't I even get a how you doing, Kelley? Where you livin'? What you doin' these days? We going straight to business?"

Cooke was silent.

Kelley chuckled again. "Listen Cooke, man, it's not like that. You know how he exaggerates everything."

"O-k-k-kay then, you tell me what it's like."

"C'mon man, let's drop that blackmail stuff." Kelley's voice grew dark and stern. "Listen to you calling him Reverend like you don't know who he really is."

"He's the pastor here whether you and I agree on it or not."

"That coward only took the job to hide so I couldn't find him when I got out." Kelley grinned nodding his head. "Actually, that was a very clever move—hiding behind a collar. And I see you're still fighting his battles for him, ain't cha?"

"He's a grown man now."

"He was a grown man then."

Cooke didn't respond. "You know, Cooke, brothers are always there for one another. Things are a little tight right now. I need a little help. You remember what that's like, don't you? Remember all the help I gave you two when you got to Detroit."

"There's a difference between getting a little help and helping yourself to somebody else's stuff."

Kelley's voice suddenly got deeper and dark. "He owes me."

"How long you gonna keep singing that sad song?"

"I spent time in jail for him."

"How do you know it was for him? No one ever proved those were his drugs, and he says they weren't."

"And you believe him?"

"No reason not to."

"They were found in his car. I was just the stupid sap that was driving it at the time. And just out of the blue I get stopped. I was set up, Cooke."

"I been hearing that so long the words ring in my ear every time I just think about you. You were set up. To this day you can't come up with a reason why Reverend would have wanted to set you up."

"Just cause I can't figure it all out doesn't mean it didn't happen."

"You're right—and it doesn't mean it did."

"Even if it wasn't a set up, it was his car and the drugs were in his car. At the very least, he lied when they asked him who the drugs belonged to. The coward. And he let me sit in that prison for six years. And I don't even know if I was the worst of what he got away with. And you always wiping up after him, like he was still a boy. Always explaining how he was traumatized by his daddy dying in the war. Well, hell! I never even had a daddy and I didn't do all the shit he did. What about that boy that died in that fight he started and ran from? That boy was trying to take up for him, and he left him there to die. I don't know what you see in him, but I know what I've seen him do, so I ain't about to call him Reverend.

By the anger in Kelley's eyes, Cooke knew that the old wound had been festering for a long time. Seemingly unmoved by his words, Cooke said, "Reverend said you're looking for fifty thousand dollars. I know you know he ain't got that kind of money."

"He's been working a lot of years, Cooke. He got retirement

funds and he's drawing a salary here and living free. Don't tell me what he ain't got," he said with a bit of exhaustion in his voice.

"I know he ain't got no fifty thousand dollars."

"Well, then maybe this needs to be a family affair. Maybe his cousin oughta help him out."

Cooke sucked air in through his teeth. He dropped his foot to the floor and leaned into Kelley's face. "Are you tryin' to blackmail me, too?"

"Listen, brotha. Brotha, brotha I ain't tryin' to hear that word. I done told you I ain't trying to blackmail anybody."

" I believe in calling a spade a spade."

"Again, I just need a little help right now to get on my feet. And you know you too have some secrets. And I've been holding on to those for you for a while. Now if you take something to the bank and ask them to hold on to it for you, they're going to charge you a fee."

"You ain't no bank."

"Maybe not. But I'm still charging the fee. I imagine between the two of you, you can come up with somethin'."

A tired Cooke leaned back into the sofa. He wasn't quite so surprised when Reverend had come to him and told him Kelley was in town trying to blackmail him. But for Kelley to now be trying to draw him into the scheme, well, the war was on. Cooke shifted gears and his expression to one more understanding. "How about we calm down over a cup of tea?"

Kelley smoothed the rim of his hat and smiled. "You still drinking that sissy drink? Naw, you know I'm allergic to tea. Ain't you got some whiskey or somethin'?"

"This is a church, Kelley," said Cooke getting up and heading towards the kitchen. "I'll make some coffee."

"Okay, if that's all you got. You know man," he called as Cooke walked away, "I sure do miss your cooking. You know that's the only reason I let you stay with me when you didn't have rent money. I knew as long as you were there, I could get a good meal." Kelley drew his hand over his mouth reminded that nothing but water had passed through it for two days. "Never could figure out how you could take two cans of beans and make a three-course meal," he said getting up and stretching.

While Cooke heated up the water in the microwave and got the cups ready, Kelley busied himself looking around Cooke's room to see what he could find. "This ain't a bad set-up you got here," he called into the kitchen. Cooke looked up without responding and Kelley continued to investigate. By the time Cooke was walking back into the room with the two cups in his hands, Kelley was just pulling one of Cooke's picture albums out of the orange crate. Cooke had enough problems with Kelley, he didn't need him looking through his photo albums finding more ammunition.

"Here," he said shoving the cup between Kelley and the album. Kelley set the album down on the crate and gratefully took the cup, eager to stop the hunger camps.

"Man, this smells good," he said settling back into the chair before he took several long sips. Cooke lifted his cup in a feigned salute and then walked back behind the sofa, drinking his coffee and watching Kelley. A couple more sips and Cooke set down his cup on the orange crate and watched and waited. It didn't take long, couldn't have been more than a couple of minutes or so. Kelley jolted straight up in his chair. "I thought you said this was coffee?"

"It is," answered Cooke coldly.

Kelley looked down at the cup and then sent it hurtling across the room crashing into a wall. "What did you put in this, Cooke?" His voice an octave higher, he jumped up from the recliner and grabbed at his throat, his eyes wide and bulging.

"I put decaf in there. Would you rather have had regular?"

"You bastard! You put tea in here. My throat is swelling. I can't breath!" Kelley patted at his pockets searching for his allergy medication and then he remembered leaving it with his girl at the motel. An attempt to race for the door only left him on his knees midway. Determined to get to his medication, he crawled over to an occupied corner and pulled himself up. Cooke sat expressionless in his chair and watched. Watched and waited until finally Kelley slid down the gray dusty wall ripping the back seam of his bright yellow pinstripe suit. A few last twitches and Kelley was still. His feet jutted out before him, his eyes bulging, and saliva dripping from his open mouth. Cooke got up and took a slow walk over to his old roommate, squatting down in front of him.

"Guess I forgot to pour out the rest of my breakfast tea before I put your coffee in that cup." Cooke reached out and lifted Kelley's limp hand and stared at the gold signet ring.

"You should have known better than to threaten me, bro-tha. Thought you knew me better than that," he ended as Kelley's wrist slipped from his fingers. Cooke reached over and closed his terror filled eyes, and then gave him a soft open-hand slap to the face. "Bro-tha," he'd said as his hand briefly rested on Kelley's cheek. He tapped his cheek one final time before standing up.

One would have thought that a lifetime of suffering through the consequences of short-term thinking would have spared Cook from this moment, but it hadn't. After having talked to Reverend earlier he knew he was going to have to take care of Kelley some way. But the decision to give him the tea was a hasty one. Not that he regretted it, but he wished he had given himself time to plan it through. Now he was stuck with a body.

This wasn't the first time in his life he had to move dead weight. He'd had to do it out at the farm a few times. But it was sure the first time he would have to do it at his age. He backed his way over to the chair Kelley had a few moments ago jumped from and sat down to think. There was no river to dump him in. No fire to burn him in and no hole to throw him in. The first time the thought of putting him in the storage area came to mind he dismissed it. But then he realized that while it wouldn't be a permanent solution, it could hold Kelley until he could take him out to the farm.

From the basement there were two ways to get him there. One meant dragging him through the back of the sanctuary of the church. And even to him that didn't seem right. The other way was twice as long, but there were fewer steps. He would have to drag Kelley down the hallway clear to the other side of the basement, which ran the whole length of the church, and then out the door that was just below the storage area. This way, at least, there was only one set of stairs.

Even though he knew no one would be there, he checked

the hall just to be sure. Kelley's body was just a few steps away so he pushed the door open wide and grabbed hold of Kelley's feet. He'd barely gotten six good steps in before he realized what he was doing was not going to work, so he went to his wardrobe and pulled out a comforter. He found some pieces of rope, laid them on the floor and put the comforter on top. With much effort, he rolled Kelley's body over onto the comforter and then used the rope to tie him up into it. He then took the ends of the rope, threw them over his shoulders and headed for the stairs. Only once did he check behind him and it was then he saw that Kelley's hat had somehow come out from under the comforter way down the hall. He reluctantly dropped the ropes and trotted back to retrieve it. There were times, like tonight, when it was difficult to distinguish the settling noises of the building and what might be the sounds of someone other than him in the building. As he picked up the hat he heard such a noise and he stopped cold dead in his tracks, tilting his head towards the way he had come. Listening. With a shaky sense of not being alone, he turned on his heel, slapping the hat against his thigh as he walked away, unknowingly knocking its peacock feather loose from the band. Once he lifted the ropes over his shoulders again he was able to regain his momentum.

Finally, he was at the storage unit. The task almost completed would have been better suited for a man half his age. At that age, he would have been able to abide the physical exertion and also keep guard on his surroundings. But he wasn't and he didn't. So he didn't see the figure that had been lurking in the area and was startled at the first sign of the night's intruders. He didn't see the figure as it backed into a dark corner and continued watching him pull and tug, and moan and groan. Cooke didn't hear the breathing as he shoved the man into the storage facility and pushed the door shut leaving out just a tip of his suit. And as he walked back down the hall towards his apartment, the feather that had fallen from Kelley's hat was no longer there, but he missed that too. If, however, he had noticed any of those things, he might have had a clue as to what happened to the body, but he didn't.

By the time Cooke got to the hospital and reached Gunther's floor, he had no more idea where to look for Kelley's body than when he began retracing his steps. His initial frustration of not knowing what happened after he returned to his room was turning into a nervous concern after realizing he had left Kelley wrapped up in his comforter.

"May I help you, sir?" asked the nurse frowning at his gauze covered finger.

"I'm looking for a friend who's supposed to be on this floor. Gunther Ferguson? He was brought in last night from a car accident."

She looked down at a spreadsheet and scanned the list. "Yes, Mr. Ferguson is in surgery right now. If you like, there is a room on the surgical floor for family."

"Surgery for what?"

"I'm sorry, sir, but I don't have that information. And even if I did, I couldn't give it out. Are you family?"

"Surgery! Did he ever regain consciousness? What floor is he on?" called Cooke over his shoulder as he headed back towards the elevator. "He's on two, sir," she called. But by the time she finished what she had to say, Cooke was on the elevator on his way up to two.

BLOOD PECKING BIRDS

Once he saw the horn-rimmed glass man, he could no longer chalk it all up to coincidence. He shouldn't have worn the shirt.

When he dialed Kitty Carlisle's phone earlier in the day she answered on the second ring, almost as if she were expecting it. "Certainly," she would come, she'd said when he explained the situation with her nephew. "I'll be on the first bus," she'd said and hung up the phone. Fifteen minutes later she called back to inform Reverend that the next bus would get her there in three hours. He agreed to meet her at the station and drive her into Becoming—almost an hour away. Ruth had begged him to send her a taxi—he was too old to drive so far out by himself, she thought. And besides, he'd spent so much of the night wrestlin' with birds he hadn't gotten enough sleep. But Reverend insisted. He didn't want his first meeting with Gunther's aunt to be among a crowd of people, just in case things went bad.

Outside of Becoming the weather was warm, the sun was brilliant. After pulling into the bus station parking lot, Reverend laid his suit coat on the backseat of the car and started across the lot. Standing center of the lot was an elevator that when taken up led to a skywalk that went over traffic to the bus station's main floor, and when taken down led under the street to the station unloading room. Ruth would have insisted that he take the elevator. But after three days of leaden skies and showers in Becoming, taking the long route across the parking lot was much more appealing. To get to Gunther's aunt, he would have to maneuver a parking lot of about two hundred cars—much larger than anything in Becoming—cross a very busy multi-lane road and walk two city blocks to get to the right entrance. But it was well worth it, he surmised. Or at least it seemed so at the time.

A strong, dry wind was shoving at him and sometimes pushed him sideways as he tried to navigate his way through the rows of cars. A few times it caused him to lose his footing and he tripped on the pebbly blacktop. As luck would have it, a particularly dirty truck was in his path and he stumbled against it. The dust on his pants leg brushed away easily, but there were pin dots of dirt on his white cotton sleeve that refused to disappear even as he scrubbed at them. He pulled his reading glasses from his shirt pocket and looked at the spots close up. For a moment he thought about returning to his car and getting his suit coat to hide the spots. But, as he thought about the distance he had crossed and the distance he had yet to go, he decided against it. He didn't want to make a bad first impression by being late. He licked his thumb a couple of times and rubbed it into his sleeve. When he realized the wetness was only making the spots worse, he began unbuttoning his cuffs. Even though she might not notice them, he would know they were there. So, he rolled up both sleeves to hide them and settled on presenting himself as looking more important than immaculate.

At the intersection, the blustery wind was emboldened by the mid-day traffic. He leaned against the light pole as he pressed the button to change the light. For some reason a feeling of frailty washed over him. He recognized it as having visited him several times recently, and he didn't like it. Not at all.

"Are you okay, sir? Can I help you across to the other side?" A young mother, with four children looking up into his face, had her hands prepped to take his elbow.

"Momma, the light is green. Let's go! We're gonna miss daddy."

"Hold on, sweetie. We need to make sure this nice man is okay. Sir?"

Reverend feigned a polite smile. "I'm fine, thank you. Please, you better hurry before the light turns red." He looked down into the face of the little girl who was prodding her mother to move more quickly. "You wouldn't wanna miss your daddy," he said, waving them on. He watched as they crossed the street, arriving at the corner just as the light turned red. The little girl, once safely on the curb, turned back and looked at him. She said something to her brother as she pointed towards him. Whatever was said, Reverend watched the little boy adjust his pants and attempt to tuck his shirt in more neatly. The mother turned around and looked at Reverend again. A look of concern spread across her face. For a brief moment, he thought they were going to come back to get him, but instead the woman placed her hand on her daughter's shoulder gently moving her forward and then they were gone.

It took a moment of mindlessly watching the cars whipping by him before Reverend acted on the fact he had yet to cross the street. He once again pressed the signal button. As he waited for the light to change, a fly began circling his head and he batted at it. But the more he batted, the more determined the fly seemed to land on him. He was relieved when the light turned green and he was able to step off the curb. But the fly was not so easily discouraged. It followed him into the intersection where, with great frustration, Reverend continued swatting. Midway across Reverend stopped. The buzzing at his ear intensified. Annoyed, he positioned himself for the kill. The fly circled his head several more times and then stopped at eye level right in front of him.

"Well, you arrogant, little, bast---!" Reverend reached out and slammed both palms together but not quick enough to catch the fly. It slipped through his palms, arched itself upwards and flew away. Reverend was caught looking up at the sky. A clear blue, cloudless sky.

When he finally heard the horns, the cars were already in the intersection and a medley of choice words were coming from the drivers' windows. It was then that the sense of déjà vu ignited such a fear in him that he was rendered enfeebled. The only part of him moving were his eyes. He scanned the cars in front of him. Each driver. Each rider. Who were they? Did they look familiar? Someone walked up behind him.

"Sir? Do you need help? Do you know where you are? Is there someone I can call? Sir? You can't stand here in the middle of the intersection, you'll get hit. Please, let me help you across."

Terror rose up in Reverend's throat and just as he opened his mouth to scream, his legs woke up and he took off running towards the bus station and away from the possibility that the horn-rimmed man was standing behind him calling down the birds. The blood pecking birds from the sky.

MS. KITTY

Down by her left foot a timid stream of blood commingled with goat's milk and orange juice. Twenty-four year old Kitty Carlisle's eyes moved down the black tiled floor past her wet ankle sock and bare calf, stopping at mid-thigh. Slowly, she began pulling back the hem of her dress. She'd just finished her period three days ago. How could she be bleeding again? The raising of her hem revealed a not so small piece of blue milk pitcher sliced into her inner thigh. Without flinching she pulled it out and studied the blood on it and the blood on her. And then her sister screamed again.

It was the barbaric ripping at the roll of flesh just above his white Sunday morning collar with her teeth that caused her father to grab Kitty by her shoulder length braids and fling her across the dinette table into the wall. But the first crack of the belt had been met by her sister with such a howl that Kitty hadn't had time to think—she just responded. And now, the ringing in her ears and the pain shooting up her spine made it difficult to move and get back across the room.

Through the chrome legs of the overturned red dinette chair in front of her, Kitty could see her sister Hazel lying on the floor across the kitchen, her face tucked in the crook of one arm, its hand covering her head, and the other arm wrapped around her slightly bulging belly. Standing over Hazel, their father wielded his razor strop welting her young eighteen-year-old flesh relentlessly.

"Leave her be, you fucking bastard!" screamed Kitty.

The piece of pitcher slipped out of Kitty's hand onto the floor and she grabbed hold of one of the chair legs to pull herself up. It was ten years ago that the quitclaim mother, the mother that gave up all legal rights to her and her sister Hazel, stood in the same doorway Hazel was now lying in. With her hands cupped under her chin, the mother's eyes were full of hope as the delivery men placed the brand new dinette set between the stove and the wall. "Don't you see, Kitty? It's the first piece of furniture we've owned that no one else has ever used. It's fresh and brand new. The only memories it will hold are the ones we make around it." And then she was gone. By the time supper was due that same day she was no where to be found. She hadn't even bothered to take her shoes, of which she only owned two pair. One pair of heels for Sunday, and a pair of flats for every other day. Both were found under her side of the bed that evening when Kitty went looking for her. Walked off bare foot as far as Kitty could tell, leaving her to make her own memories dealing with the abuse Quitclaim fled.

By the time Kitty finally got to her feet, the screaming had stopped. The voice behind the banging on the front door threatening to break it down if somebody didn't open it while the felon stooped over her sister still holding the bloodied strop. Cheese grits had been a demand of the felon for breakfast that morning and they sat on the back burner of the stove next to fresh pork sausage, an occasional bubble popping through to the surface. Undeterred by the fact the pot was hot, Kitty picked up the grits from the stove and headed across the room, slipping and sliding all the way. The kitchen was only twelve feet square, but it might as well have been a mile square for the time it took her to get there sliding through spilt milk and juice and blood and grease and all the time pictures going through her head of all the horrible memories the dinette set held since Quitclaim ran away. All of the screaming and the beatings and the yelling. And all the misery. The day to day misery of it all. She was tired of feeling like she couldn't get enough air in her lungs. She was tired of sitting in the hollowed out rotted tree in the woods screaming till her throat was raw. And now after spending all of her life up to this point trying to keep her safe, her sister lay dead on the kitchen floor with her murderer slumped over her as if he had no idea what he had done—still shouting at the limp body. So when she lifted the hot pot of grits, she was just trying to silence the noise. Make him shut the fuck up. When she slammed it against the side of his head it knocked him down to his knees. Stunned, he looked up at her sideways as he reached up to touch the blood coming from his ear. But instead of him being quieted, he began shouting again—at her this time. So, she raised the pot again, grits dripping down her arm and took aim. But the second time a hand caught her in mid swing.

"Let it go, girl! Now let it go!"

After an unsuccessful battle to keep the pot in hand, she fell to the floor and crawled over to her sister whose face was now laying in a puddle of vomit. The same hands that had taken the pot now held her by her shoulders and were pulling her away from Hazel.

"No!" she screamed. "He killed her! That black bastard killed her!" She snatched herself out of the hands and grabbed hold of Hazel pulling her out of the puddle and towards her, finally resting her head in her lap as she braced herself against a cabinet door.

"Hazel, Hazel," she cried rocking her sister's head back and forth, "I'm so sorry."

Hazel groaned.

"Sister! You ain't dead? You ain't dead!" cried Kitty through lips covered in snot and tears. "I thought you were dead for sure." Kitty suddenly realized the small kitchen was filled with people—neighbors—some from as far as a quarter mile away. They began pulling at her again trying to separate her from Hazel.

"You gotta let us take her," one woman said. "If we don't get her to the hospital, she will be dead."

Finally Kitty let go and watched as Hazel was swept up by one of the men and hurried away. Her father had already been taken out and the woman once again stooped down beside her.

"Honey we gotta get you up."

"No, I just wanna be left alone."

Then from the other side of her, "Kitty, it's Hattie. We gotta get this mess cleaned up before the sheriff gets here. They liable to take you away if we don't get you up."

"Go away, Hattie. Leave me alone!"

"You're bleeding. We need to get you to the hospital, too."

"Leave me alone, leave me alone, leave me alone!" And suddenly a scream erupted from Kitty that would not be controlled. It seemed to bubble up all the way down from her toes and she was forced to open her mouth and let it have its way with her. It wasn't until she didn't see or hear anyone else that she finally stopped screaming. But it was a much longer time before she got up from the floor. By the time she finished crying, it was noon and the sausage was too dried out to eat.

"Ms. Carlisle?"

When Kitty turned and looked at him, Reverend supposed she looked like Gunther's mother would have looked if she were still alive. Earlier on the phone she had made an offhand remark that she was crashin' into eighty. But Reverend wouldn't have guessed it. Her brandy-colored face was framed by the whitest of gray hair pulled tightly back in a bun. Light, insignificant lines were sprinkled across her face—around her eyes, the corners of her mouth, one across her forehead. Slight of build she had broad shoulders and stood about five foot six. She wore a gray pair of pants and a pink flowered sweater.

"You my Gunther's pastor? The one who called?"

"Yes, ma'am, I am."

She reached down to pick up her brown Louis Vuitton bag.

"Can I take that for you?" Reverend asked as he reached towards the bag.

"No, thank you. I can manage," she said pulling the bag close to her body. There was an awkward silence, each one searching the other for some flashback that never came.

"Well, shall we go then?" Reverend gestured towards the hallway behind him.

"Shouldn't we be going that way?" Kitty pointed to the street beyond the window glass she had been remembering through.

Reverend shifted on his feet mumbling and looked down at the floor. "No, ma'am. I think it's safer if we go through the tunnel. There's an elevator that'll take us straight to the parking lot. The traffic this time of day is terrible." He took two steps and turned waving at her to follow him.

It wasn't until they reached the car that Kitty finally let the bag go. She slid into the front passenger seat and allowed him to store it safely in the trunk of his car. The first few moments after pulling out into traffic were quiet—awkwardly so.

Once away from the airport traffic, Reverend began patting at his shirt pocket and then remembered he had left the two books from Gunther's bedroom in his jacket pocket in the backseat of the car.

"I don't remember Gunther ever mentioning you before. How long has it been since you were back in Becoming?"

"I haven't set foot back there since I left."

Reverend watched from the corner of his eye as Kitty picked at the roll of stocking that was knotted just above her knee.

"Oh. Not even for your sister's funeral?"

"No." She turned and looked at him as if to say something, but then returned to gazing out the passenger window.

Silence.

"Well, then," he said awkwardly, "I thought we'd drop your suitcase at Gunther's and give you some time to rest. I'll come back for you later and take you over to the hospital."

"I'd prefer to go straight to the hospital. I came to see Gunther. I can rest when I get back home. Take me on to the hospital, please."

"If you're sure."

"I'm sure. I'd like to be there when he wakes up."

Reverend tapped his index fingers nervously on the steering wheel as they drove another half mile. He turned on the radio to fill some of the quiet that had been so welcome on his way to the bus station, but was now uncomfortable.

"What's he like?" Reverend strained to hear her question as she continued to stare out the window. Then she turned and asked again. "You said he's worked for you sometime now. What's he like, this nephew of mine?"

Reverend took his time, choosing his words carefully. "I've come to think of him as family now, I suppose. But I was hoping you'd be able to shed some light on him, actually." He chuckled nervously and then cleared his throat. "Well now, let me think," he replied, and then paused as he flicked on his turn signal while making a right turn onto the two-lane highway back to Becoming. "First I'd have to say he's a very private person. He doesn't talk about himself or his family. I'd never even been to his house until today to find your phone number. And as a pastor, you learn not to pry with folks like Gunther."

"Like Gunther?"

"The quiet, introverted type. He seems content at Promisekeepers and we're happy to have him there. Wouldn't want to drive him away. He's quiet. Pleasant, but not easy to get to know. At least that's been my experience of him. He comes in and does his work and leaves. Unless we need him for something in the evening, we generally don't see him around the church again until the next morning. I tell you, though, he's one of the kindest people you'll ever meet. We have a good number of homeless people who come in for a meal each day—stay to get out of the weather. I've watched him with those folks. He's particularly gentle with the older ones, the sicklier ones. Very, very friendly with them. Which has always made me confused about why he doesn't seem to have any friends. He ever talk to you about friends he might have here?"

"We only talk on the phone every few years. I think sometimes he just wants to know if I've remembered anything about his father."

"Did you know his father?"

"No. And I'm not sure his mother did either."

"Meaning?"

"She went to a party one night and came home pregnant. She was drugged and raped."

Reverend noticed the sky was beginning to gray as they moved closer to Becoming. He reached over and slid the knob to allow fresh air through the vents. Suddenly he realized his left hand was gripping the steering wheel too tightly. Without trying to sound horrified, he asked, "So Gunther is a product of rape?"

"Yes."

"Does he know?"

"Of course not. And he never will," she warned.

"No, of course, I would never tell him something like that. Did she know the man?"

"Yes. Maybe. I don't know. All I know is that she asked

to go to a party that night. Our father was very strict and we didn't go out to parties or anything else. She was eighteen and she begged me to help her. So I made up a lie to tell my daddy about how she and I were going to some church event or other. It took me a full week of asking, but he finally agreed and off she went. Some boy from out of the city was there and she had fallen head over heels with him. It never occurred to me something like that would happen. I found her laying in the front yard later that night. She was groggy and couldn't tell me what happened. But when she woke up the next day, she was different. Her brain seemed to have come unwired. And then a few weeks later we found out she was pregnant. Some men gathered and went looking for the boy, but couldn't find him. Which is probably a good thing. They would have killed that poor boy for sure if they had."

Reverend cleared his throat again. "Tell me. What was she like before it happened?"

"We were five years apart. I guess by the time she came, I was just needing someone to be with. Both my parents worked long hours so I would find myself making my own dinner at night, doing homework at the kitchen table alone. I only had my dolls. So I was better than excited when she showed up. Everything she asked for, I tried to get for her. I remember I worked to earn money to get her a doll she saw in one of the shop windows when she was six. She would just talk about that doll all the time. She even named it while it sat in that window. 'Can we go see Sadie?' she would ask." Kitty chuckled lightly. I bought her that doll too. When I gave it to her, it wasn't Christmas or even her birthday."

Through static signal, the radio announcer was trying to tell them about a mattress sale that was happening but he was interrupted by the weather person who cut in to talk about how the sun was going to hang around for a while and there would be good weather for the civic center event coming up in two days.

"By the time she was six she could recite all of the states and their capitals. By the time she was ten, she could recite the presidents in order. She loved music. She would sing from sun up to sun down. She would even sing herself to sleep at night."

"Sounds like you loved her very much."

"Very."

"But still you didn't come to her funeral."

"Too much guilt for leaving them behind. My momma left her and then I left her. I did try to make it right, though. But she was convinced that boy was coming back for her. She would sit on that front porch every evening just waiting. Waiting for him to come take her away. Gunther told me once when he was young that she had gotten it in her head that his daddy had returned to Becoming and was living on the streets and just didn't know how to find her. Crazy. Becoming ain't big enough to get lost in. She spent all of her years lookin' in the streets for that man. I even sent her a bus ticket once after our father died. Of course she wouldn't come. Not even for a visit. Eventually I realized people gotta live what they gotta live. I found my momma some years back. She was living the same black and blue life she had escaped with our daddy. You see? It didn't matter where she lived, her life was gonna be the same. I could have made Hazel come, but it wouldn't have changed her life."

"Did he? Ever come back?"

"You don't come back for a woman you raped."

Reverend felt his cowardice kick in as he propped his elbow up on the door sill and rubbed the back of his head. There were just ten minutes left to drive.

"Pull over."

"Are you okay? Somethin' wrong, Ms. Kitty?"

"Pull over. Just pull over. Please."

Reverend gently guided the car to a stop in the gravel edge of the road. He'd barely put the car in park when she opened the door and got out. He too got out and looked over the hood of the car at her. He could tell when he looked at her face she knew it too. She was staring up at the ominous clouds hanging over Becoming and then turned around looking behind her and all around her.

"Did you know it looked like that?"

Reverend walked around the car and stood by her side. "It's difficult to see anything when you're standing in the middle of it. But yes, I knew." The sound of a distant motor behind them prompted Reverend to take Kitty's arm to help her back to the car.

"We probably should get going."

"What in God's name have you all done?"

Startled and at a loss for words at the question, Reverend looked over at the approaching vehicle, and there he was, the horn-rimmed glass man riding as smooth as you please in a dark blue Toyota Camry kicking up road dust as he came.

He guided his car to the side of the road just in front of Reverend's car and stepped out. Reverend's grip tightened on Kitty's arm.

"Are you two okay? Having car trouble?"

Reverend didn't answer.

"No, we were just lookin' at the sky. We're fine," replied Kitty.

The man looked up and then looked back at Kitty. "Looks like trouble's brewing over there. Well, if you're certain you're fine…"

"Yes, thank you for stopping."

He looked at Reverend with a raised brow before hurrying back into his car—and then he was gone. Reverend released his hand from Kitty's arm and hurried back to his side of the car. As he lay his foot on the running board he looked over the hood at the second witness just as a knowing smile spread across her face. Just before she slipped into the seat, from the corner of his eye Reverend could have sworn he saw a smile in her eyes. And just as he heard the muffled thump of the car door closing, the first droplets of blood pierced through the woven fabric of his clean, bright white button down dress shirt.

JULIA

When she finally got home, she'd changed out of her work clothes and put on a dress. She'd brushed back her wavy dark auburn hair and shoved it into a oyster shell hair clip. She'd spent an hour with a cold compress over her eyes to take away the swelling and redness. And she'd left the toothpick in her thigh.

Now, Julia stood peering into a vending machine on the first floor of the hospital, wondering with great anxiety where they had moved the almond chocolate bars. She had been standing in the dimly lit concession room for more than fifteen minutes afraid to go and afraid to stay. It had been a difficult task talking Cooke into believing over the phone that she was sick enough to have to leave him with Carlita to prepare for the dinner crowd. But she needed to be at the hospital in case Gunther needed her. And if it meant being caught in a lie, then so be it.

The chocolate bar was for Gunther. Sometimes when he was done with his work around the church, he would have one with a soda and sit and chat with the diners. Occasionally, but not too often, she would buy one to share, setting it on one of the stainless steel kitchen rolling carts so he could see it while walking by and ask who it belonged to. And she could say, "Me," and "You're welcome to share it if you like." Sometimes—often—he would ask her to take a break, get off her feet and sit with him so they could eat their halves at the same time. But most of the time, she would politely refuse pointing out a pot to be washed or sponges to be bleached. She almost never obliged him. Because if she was near him often, eventually he would know her scent—who she was and where she'd been. He'd see it in her eyes that he was the one she thought of in the dark as her hands warmed her thighs and made her moan out loud. She didn't want that. Particularly since their last encounter. She didn't want him to think she wanted more than he could offer.

He had explained once that being single was a choice. At least for now, anyway. There were things he was committed to, a promise he wanted to keep, people who needed caring for. He had implied the people were the ones that came into the kitchen. But she knew differently.

The coin return button blinked relentlessly at her demanding she either make a selection or take her five quarters back. She pressed the button. There was another vending machine on the intensive care floor. She would look for the chocolate bar with almonds there.

When she got to his floor, the elevator opened to a busy four o'clock shift change. Nurses in light blue scrubs flew back and forth from their stations filling small white paper cups with pills of pink and blue and red and then delivering them to their patients while introducing the night staff and saying toothy goodbyes. "You'll be fine, sweetie. Your night nurse will take good care of you and I'll see you in the morning. Okay, dear?"

Before she even stepped off the elevator, Julia began scanning the hall for Cooke's bent figure and Reverend's erect one.

"Julia? I didn't see your name on the schedule for tonight. Did you get your days mixed up?" Doris, the night floor supervisor was headed towards her, wrapping her stethoscope around her neck and then checking her afro with a few quick pats with finger slayed hands.

"Julia?" This time her name tasted like chocolate and almonds. But it couldn't have been him. He was in the intensive care ward. Her eyes darted around the hallway. She was certain she had just heard him call her, though.

"No," she mumbled, still scanning the hallway. "I didn't get my days mixed up."

"You okay, sugar?" The supervisor's eyebrows lowered in a concerned frown.

"A friend—a co-worker, was in an accident last night and I'm here to check on him. Gunther Ferguson is his name. Do you know where he... ?" And then suddenly there he was, turning a corner and headed straight towards her.

Julia jammed her hand down into her purse in search of a lie to tell Cooke. She dug down past a leather wallet filled with expired credit cards and insignificant photos, and down past the coupon holder with coupons that expired months ago and for things she would never use like pink razors and canned oysters. Way past all of that and her hair brush, nail file, polish and gum. And just before she began scratching at the bottom of her purse, she paused for just a split second resting her hand on her sage smudge stick, tempted to take it out and light it.

"I'm just comin' on duty, but I can check for you. What did you say his name was?"

"Ferguson. Gunther Ferguson."

"Got it. Girl, you don't look so good. I was just headed to the desk. Come on and walk with me."

"I thought you were sick," he said. And there he was standing four feet in front of her, his face full of anger. The clarity of his voice was startling.

Julia felt the blood drain from her face and she quickly dropped her eyes. She'd never encountered him outside of Promisekeepers. She had made sure of that with all of his black smoke streaming from his pores and billowing from his mouth. She used her smudge stick every morning before entering Promisekeepers and never looked at him fearing if she looked up she too would become black smoke.

"Well, I was right about you not looking good. Baby, you sick? You know you shouldn't be here if you're sick. Even if you were on the schedule for tonight, which thank goodness you aren't. But if you're sick, you need to go home."

"I'm not sick," she said forcefully.

"That's not what you told me a few hours ago."

"Well, I'm not sick anymore, and I wanted to come see about Gunther."

Without acknowledging Cooke's intrusion into their conversation, Doris continued her gentle reprimand. "To be on the safe side, Julia, I want you to go downstairs and get checked out. You won't be able to stay up here if you're sick, but you know that already. Okay, then." Doris took a step back. "I gotta get back to work. And make sure you check the schedule before you leave, hear? Don't want you comin' in when you're not scheduled to be..."

"You work here?" Cooke asked accusingly.

Doris had started to walk away but then turned back. She didn't know the man in Julia's face, but she didn't like his tone. Julia was one of her favorite workers. She'd found her particularly gentle to the sickest of the patients, the terminally ill, the end of lifers. And particularly kind to the indigent who weren't allowed to stay for any extended time, but cast out due to lack of insurance. Julia always suggested places for them to get help, places to stay, places they might be taken in. And on occasion, even against hospital policy, offering to take them there. So even though it was against Human Resource's rules, Doris felt compelled to stand up for Julia.

"She's one of our stellar employees," she replied matter of factly. "It's like she was born for it." Doris flashed a big reassuring smile at Julia and then added, "I'm serious about you getting checked out. And if you still want me to check on your friend, bring a slip back with you." Then, with a brief wave of the hand she headed down the hall already answering questions and yelling orders.

"Why you keep the fact you're workin' here such a big secret?"

"Just because you don't know don't mean it's a secret."

"But, how come I didn't know? You been working at Promisekeepers for a long time now. How come I didn't know you worked at the hospital? What do you do here? You a nurse?"

"No, I'm not a nurse, I just… "

And it was then that she thought she'd found the lie, and wrapping her fingers around it she yanked her hand out of her purse, out past the red frayed coin purse and checkbook, out past a roll of wintergreen lifesavers and a newly acquired wallet, and suddenly her five quarters were flying through the air and bouncing across the floor. And as she watched them rolling into corners and under the counter, she caught a glimpse of something else she had yanked out of her purse. A feather. A brown feather that floated in a "see me, see me" kind of way, rocking back and forth, back and forth gently on the hospital's sterile air ever so slowly. She reached for it, but Cooke was faster and snatched it up in his hand. Through the haze of black smoke she watched as he lifted it up between the two of them and twirled it easily between his fingers.

Finally she broke the prolonged silence.

"That belongs to me," she said looking down and holding her hand out.

"Does it?"

Julia stared at Cooke's hand for a few moments trying to decide if she was fast enough to snatch the feather out of it. But then she simply turned to walk away.

"Where else have you been that I don't know about?"

Before she could think of a reply, the elevator doors opened again and out stepped Reverend holding the elbow of a woman.

"Perfect timing." Reverend smiled awkwardly at Cooke and looked at Julia. "Ms. Julia, I'm surprised to find you here."

"So was I," said Cooke.

"I was going to get something from the vending machine,"

mumbled Julia while trying to retrieve the nearest quarters.

"Just a minute, don't be off so quickly. Especially since you were the one to point me in the direction of Ms. Kitty here."

Julia allowed herself to be distracted from gathering her coins to focus on Gunther's mysterious aunt who had gone away too soon for Gunther to describe her in one of their chocolate breaks. It was not natural for her to so quickly and so willingly look into the face of an unknown, but Ms. Kitty seemed to have brought something to the room that was calming or reassuring, or both. "Ms. Kitty, this here is Ms. Julia. She works in the kitchen at my church. And this here is my cousin Cooke, named so because he's so good at it. He's the cook at Promisekeepers. Has been since before I got there." Kitty stepped forward pulling her glasses down off her nose. She leaned in and looked at Cooke. She looked back at Reverend and then again at Cooke. She pressed her glasses back up and then said with the greatest sense of revelation, "Well, I'll be."

The thunder rattled the hospital windows. Cooke lifted his bandaged hand and pressed it to his chest. Reverend shifted nervously in his shoes.

"I didn't know anyone besides Gunther here in Becoming knew or remembered me. I'm curious how you knew to contact me. Don't get me wrong. I'm very grateful. Just curious. You two must be pretty good friends."

"He must have mentioned you in a conversation or something," replied Julia. "I really don't remember." As she was talking, she looked over at Cooke who was still holding the feather in his hand. They locked eyes and he slowly stuffed the feather down into his coat pocket.

"Ms. Kitty, let's get you settled over there in the waiting room. I've got to call my wife and let her know I've made it back."

"You don't need to call her."

"Huh?"

"She's here. Got here about twenty minutes ago. She went to find the bath—" And then on queue, Ruth was coming down the hall.

The vending machine was in the family waiting room, and as the four settled in, Julia stood at the machine again hunting the chocolate bar with almonds.

"Ms. Kitty, G-g-gunther's gonna be in there a while. You have plenty of time to go back to Reverend's and get unpacked."

"Oh, no," she replied. "I had hoped I could stay at Gunther's. It's been a long time since I've been home. Unless, of course, you think he would mind…" The three looked around at each other not knowing how to answer the question.

"Well," Reverend said, "seeing as you lived there before he did, I guess there'd be no harm in it. I have his keys so I can let you in."

"Perfect."

"Reverend, I still have some errands to run," said Ruth. Ms. Kitty, if you don't mind, I can drop you off at the house so you can rest a bit. Reverend can come and pick you up later and bring you back. It looks like it's going to be a long evening. I chatted just briefly with the nurse. They are expecting him to be in recovery for quite some time."

After a bit of discussion, Kitty agreed and headed off with Ruth.

Cooke grabbed hold of Reverend's elbow. "Did you know she worked here?" Julia had chosen a seat near the window away from the smoke.

"Who?"

"Her. Julia."

"Well... no. No, I didn't know you worked here, Ms. Julia. I'm surprised we haven't run into each other before."

"I only work in the evenings."

Reverend looked mildly surprised. "Well, that makes sense then. Cooke, don't look so disturbed. The folks that work at Promisekeepers have other lives, too, just like you and me. Not our business what they do outside of the church. We can't know everything about 'em. Heck, Cooke, what do we know about Gunther? And if I should know about anybody at Promisekeepers, I should know about Gunther. Shouldn't I? Look at us. Old men. What do we know, Cooke? What do we know?"

HOME AGAIN, HOME AGAIN, JIGGETY-JIG

There was no blood and grits smeared across a brown and orange linoleum floor like a Basquiat painting, nor any other thing in the silent kitchen that bore resemblance to her memories. Kitty dropped her suitcase in the doorway and in all gentleness as to not wake up the dead, she walked across the floor guided by one pointed, thin finger. She stood perfectly still noticing the delicacy of the sheer curtains above the window in front of her with a relief so complete at having not experienced any of the possible emotions that she'd anticipated upon entering the house that she had abandoned just like the Quitclaim mother.

The agony she had born for so long for having left her sister had been sharp and deep, but now looking through these curtains into a clear unencumbered glass, she knew nothing would have been had by staying. Maybe her mother had known that too.

She pulled her sweater more tightly around her shoulders and then lifted a corner of the curtain peering out through the crystal glass window continuing to notice Gunther's life, wondering how many times someone else had stood here, looking out, wondering about the life behind them and in front of them. There was a small deck with a couple of deck chairs, redwood with blue and white striped cushions—new since she'd lived here. Beyond the deck were islands of brown things shooting up from the ground sectioned off by gray cement pavers. Brown branches, brown leaves, brown bushes, all striving to be again. The entire view from this window was different from what she remembered.

She remembered fondly the chicken coop that so many years ago had adorned the yard and the day she remembered that the chicks she thought were purchased for her morning companionship were actually meant for evening meals. She remembered a clothes line heavy with little girls dresses and panties and darned socks. And the way the wind blew her mother's delicate slips up like ghostly apparel. She remembered the games of hide and seek and the hand jive, and "bubblegum bubblegum in a dish" played with a sister she had cherished like a favorite doll.

Standing there, she had run so deeply into the past that when Ruth first came and stood beside her, it didn't sink in until later that Ruth had said she'd found the thermostat and turned off the air conditioning, and that she didn't understand why it was on anyway. And when Ruth asked about the framed photo of the woman and child on the wall—who they were and if it was her—she barely glanced at the photo before responding that no, it was her sister and Gunther. Then, by the time she had returned to the day, Ruth had gone and the sun had started to go down behind a yard of dead things.

TIMING IS EVERYTHING

The fetid smell woke her up. Kitty had only intended to catch her breath for a moment on the sofa, but now it was an hour later. The room had warmed to a comfortable temperature and she slipped off her sweater. The smell, though. It was wretched. So the first ten minutes up from her nap were spent searching for the smell. She sniffed every possible cause of the nuisance she could think of, the dirty clothes hamper sitting under a rattan shelf in a corner of the bathroom, the pink toilet bowl, and the refrigerator. She finally decided that it was not on the first floor at all, but coming up from the basement, which would make perfect sense if that was still the place the garbage cans were kept, just inside the garage door. But this new revelation only instigated another search—looking for the key to the basement door.

So for the next half hour she looked everywhere she could think of for the key. But so far, it was nowhere to be found. From one room to the other she had gone, starting in the kitchen, peering into cupboards and rifling through drawers, and working back to the bedrooms, poking into jewelry boxes and patting dresser and table tops. She hunted until every cupboard and drawer had been searched. Every end table, every closet and coat pocket she could find. So far, she had found a strange assortment of everything. A cobalt blue bottle of Eau de something or another had been snuggly shoved into the back corner of a dresser drawer. The power of its fragrance long since waned. There was a stack of men's magazines dating back more than thirty years hidden under a loose floorboard in Gunther's bedroom closet. Her cane had accidentally discovered them while she poked around the closet shelves. It had taken some maneuvering to get down on her knees and pull the stack out of the narrow slit. But after she did, with a cynical chuckle she shoved them back in their hole and slammed the board closed. She had found some odd things during her search, but not the key. Not the damned key!

Finally, she called Reverend.

The timing of Kitty's phone call would have seemed like divine intervention for Reverend had he not been so consumed with guilt when interrupted. Ruth had been standing over him as he sat on one of the sofas in the family room of the hospital. She was shoving a photo in his face that she said she'd taken off the wall at Gunther's.

"Who is this?"

Reverend had leaned up on the edge of the sofa, looking back at Cooke, his eyes wide and questioning why the photo meant anything to his wife.

Cooke's response was to push himself up off the sofa with his good hand and declare his need to get his prescription.

"After I get my meds, I've gotta go c-c-check on the ki-ki-

kitchen," he'd said. "I'll be back. But if anything happens, call me." And then he was gone down the hall.

It was just then that the nurse called Reverend to the phone.

"Yes," he said, "I can come right away." And then, "The hospital is asking for proof of insurance. I assume it's probably in Gunther's wallet, but I couldn't find it when I was there earlier. Would you mind looking while I'm on my way?"

Although Kitty didn't remember seeing it earlier, she assured Reverend that she would look for it and bring it along with her if she found it. So when she hung up the phone, she took off for the next hunt.

HOVERING 2—
NEW HAIRS

Even now his concern for his mother had not waned. Her disconsolate spirit was crushing. There was no question he was no longer the keeper of her. He was no longer her savior.

Over his shoulder, he could feel a presence. He recognized it as the same one he'd felt while in the confines of the body. And as then, the presence was guiding, helping him to understand.

"Can I help her?"

"No. All of the helping is over. It's time for her to make her own decisions, however difficult they may be."

"But she needs me. I've always taken care of her. Good care. There's never been anyone but me."

"Before you, I am."

"Then… why? Why can't she move to the light?"

"It's her choice. As I have been there to guide you, she too has been guided. It's not her earthly life that holds her back. It is her inability to let go of it."

"Does she know this is what she is choosing? Certainly

not." He remembered her long nights, which became their long nights and felt darkness begin to surround him.

The day had passed with all the normalcy of their other Saturdays. Its corners scoured with bulging eyeballs, and then attacked on covered hands and knees with twisted butter knives. Scraped, poked and prodded to give up any little bitty, itsy witsy nasty thing that had found its way there since the last time it had been gone over. Its liquids were painful. Ammonia and bleach. But better in the air than on his skin turning his bath water into acid as had happened so many times before. Seeping into his body through the bottomless dark holes and scratches the Watkin's bristle brush through time had left over him and in him. But not as much on this day. The bathroom was, for the most part, now off limits to her when he was in there in any state of disrobe—be it fully or partially. Now that he was officially a teenager. Now, since he had grown hair. Unexpected hairs in unexpected places. At least unexpected to him and her. They would not have been unexpected to his father, though, but he was not there. If he had known it was only necessary to grow unexpected hairs in unexpected places he would have willed himself to do it long ago. Closed his eyes and pushed them out one by one.

This particular day she stood outside the door calling, "Gunther? Gunther? You scrubbin' in there? You gettin' clean?"

To which he answered, "Yes, Momma," through a lie of ammonia poured into a washcloth laid beside the bathroom door so she would smell it and be satisfied. It wouldn't have done him any good to put the burning liquid in the water with him anyway. His skin had been scrubbed so intensely for so many years that it was almost impenetrable. Like that of an alligator.

By noon the two and a half loads of wash that she had put through the wringer and pinned to dry on an early morning line were thrown in a basket and set beside the floor drain in the basement. Once there by the drain, she wet them again. Slinging water at them from the sprinklin' bottle, and then folding them tightly and shoving them back down into the basket, but even more tightly so they would stay moist until they were hit with the pressing iron.

There by the drain was where Gunther had always witnessed her falling into herself. Disappearing and someone else showing up in her flesh. He was never able to see what she saw down there, or hear what she heard. Not even when she would leave the room and he would lie down beside it pulling the cover up and calling out, "Who's in there? You come out of there and bring my momma back! You hear! Bring her back!"

But now as he hovered he could hear the echo of voices that day as they called from deep in the drain—louder and louder. He watched as in the middle of her task she set the iron back on its heel and stared down at the drain. Down in that covered hole where the water went down clear and pure with rainbow thinned bubbles, but came up choking with smelly, dirty rot. She stared until he called her name and then she threw a powder from a green and gold can that promised to make your drains run free down into the hole. But it only ran clear again for a short while. Just until the rot built back up to the top.

The last bleached T-shirt took the longest to finish, with the voice getting louder and all. It took three good pressings before she finally stopped creasing the same long wrinkle in the front of the shirt. But finally finished, she folded the shirt in thirds, one side over and then the other. And then in thirds again from top to bottom and then laid it on the ready to put away pile and looked up at him with eyes longing to just be able to sit down and rest. But instead, she motioned for him to put away her pressing things after he finished putting away the clothes, and she headed for the stairs. The house was in order, from top to bottom. It was time for her to get cleaned up.

Bright candy apple red and dessicate, she scratched the tarnished tube of lipstick across an expectant mouth, flooding raw, cracked lines with each stroke as he stood in the hall doorway and watched. Bits of red dotted the marble top of her dressing table and she swiped at them, smearing them and then eventually clearing them away with a balled up piece of tissue. One by one she removed the six pins that held her hair in a bun and laid them in a small crystal dish. Beside the comb and brush it was the only other thing that found a home on her dressing table. After the final pin was laid neatly aside, she picked up her brush and began brushing with long definite strokes. One, two, three... she counted until all one hundred strokes were completed and her hair glistened. Then she set the brush back in the exact same spot she had taken it from and placed her folded hands in her lap and gazed into the mirror. He always wondered what it was she saw when she looked in that mirror. By then he could tell it was no longer her. She had been swallowed up in one of those deep red fissures long before one hundred.

"Momma? Momma? Where you going, Momma?"

She turned in his direction and then turned slowly back like a ballerina in a music box whose insides got stuck and only allowed her half the rotation. She never uttered a word going clockwise or counter. She just gazed off into somewhere he was never invited. It was always enough, though, for him to know that no matter where she went, she could always hear his voice when he called.

She got up from her seat and gently picked up a pair of freshly ironed white gloves and a black patent leather purse she had set out on the edge of her bed. She brushed by him as she headed into the hallway. "Set my gardenin' tools out for me, baby," she'd said, "and be sleep when I get home, you hear?" she whispered softly as she stood on her tiptoes to give him a kiss goodbye.

Normally he would have quickly responded with a "Yes, ma'am," but this time it didn't come so quickly. And as she slid into the front seat of the red Ford pick-up truck that Ms. Annie had given her cause her husband had died three weeks after he bought it and she had no use for it, he had wondered why it had taken him so long to realize his new hairs gave him the ability to say yes or no. And that night was a no.

A SMELL

Like a cavalcade of skeletons, lightning rattled across the sky, the storm wailed with a deafening intensity, and Reverend lay face down and bleeding in the mud feeling exposed and defenseless.

All the way to Gunther's house he had asked himself the question, "How bad could a smell be?" The question made him recall a drunk that frequented the church cafeteria a year or so back and how they would often make him bathe before he sat down and ate. But Reverend didn't think that even his odor would permeate an entire house. But he allowed Kitty's urgency to become his own, so much so that the impracticality of walking around in Gunther's backyard in slick-soled shoes on wet blacktop in pitch darkness never occurred to him. If it had, he wouldn't be in his current situation.

The last thing he remembered was getting his flashlight out of the glove compartment and stepping out of the car. He vaguely remembered his foot had caught on something just a few steps away and had sent him tumbling, flashlight flying out of his hand.

The deck light flicked on.

The smell of wet earth filled his nostrils and he spit it and pieces of gravel from his mouth, tasting a bit of blood with each flick of his tongue. He struggled to push himself up on stinging hands. Up and soaked from head to toe, he grabbed hold of the open car door to steady himself. And that's when he thought he saw it the first time. Out just at the edge of the treeline something shimmered. His foot slipped and he grabbed more tightly at the car door. When he looked back out into the yard whatever he had seen was gone. He blinked and wiped at his face looking anxiously around one more time. Glancing occasionally over his shoulder, he headed towards the garage door where he hoped to find Gunther's garbage cans filled with leftovers and needing to be set out.

When he finally reached the door and got the right key in the lock, the stench that rushed out from inside when he pulled the door up almost made him vomit. He took a couple of steps into the garage, a face full of rain and mud. He was agitated not to find a light switch just inside the door, but fortunately the garbage cans were. Single-mindedly, he grabbed the first and yanked up the lid. Empty. He dropped the lid to the floor and it bounced and landed just under the garage door. He opened the second can. It too was empty. He shoved the lid back down and took the four steps towards the runaway lid. As he reached down to pick it up a glint of something caught his eye. His first instinct was to ignore it. But a second glance stopped him in his tracks. The lid slipped from his hand and rested silently on the cement floor. A ring, lying on the garage door threshold glinted at him and he picked it up, stepping backwards into the garage away from the rain. He stared at it, rolling it in his fingers and looking for the inscription—knowing he would find it but hoping that he wouldn't. There couldn't possibly be another man's ring that bore the number three as its center stone. And there it was—inside, he read the inscription as if it were brand new. "Till the end." Wording that never felt as ominous before. His ring was in the bottom of a drawer somewhere. He hadn't seen Cooke's in years. The only one he had seen recently was the one that was on the finger of the witness the night before. He looked out into the yard. The rain was still whipping violently. The lightening was still cracking across the sky. But someone had turned the sound off. How had the witness's ring got into Gunther's garage? Did he have something to do with Gunther's accident? Had Cooke lied and met the witness and somehow gotten his ring and dropped it here when he came looking for Gunther?

He looked out into the yard. There it was again—just beyond where he had fallen. A shimmering. A figure. He squinted and called out, "Hey! Who's out there?" He glanced quickly down at the ring, and then called out in disbelief, "Kelley, is that you?" He gripped the ring more tightly. With the next flash of lightening things became more confusing. This time, he was sure he recognized the figure, and with a voice of deep disbelief he whispered, "Gunther?" He started to step out for a clearer look when someone shouted his name from behind and he jolted around. There was no one there. No witness staring at him through eyes of accusation and whispering threats. No one. The hairs on the back of his neck stood up. He turned around stepping back out into the rain, frantically looking out into the night, certain this time who he had seen.

"Gunther!" No answer. He clutched the top of his drenched coat around his throat too afraid to move.

The shimmering was gone, and no matter how narrow he made his eyes, nor how much rain he swiped away from them, there was nothing to see. Another noise coming from behind him. He turned slightly to face it. It wasn't until then that he noticed Gunther's truck pulled into the back of the garage. And in a small, unsure way he felt relieved. It was not uncommon for Gunther to pick up something late at night to be delivered to the church in the morning. And he'd been gone for almost twenty-four hours now. It was clear where the smell was coming from. He took one last look out into the darkness and then backed out of the rain. He moved along the wall up the left side of the truck. Just a few steps in he was able to see a light switch and a door. He reached the switch and turned it up. No light. Feeling somehow betrayed, he angrily flicked the switch up and down, up and down enough times to realize it wasn't coming on. But standing this close to the truck, he knew by his gag reflexes that this had to be where the smell was coming from. He walked back around to the back of the truck. As always there was a black tarp that covered its bed. It kept the produce and groceries safe from the elements during morning and evening pickups. And as always, it was tied down at all four corners. The knots were tight and it took some doing for Reverend to get the first undone. As he began untying the knot on the opposite corner, he thought he saw something moving underneath the tarp up towards the cabin. He paused, and when he did the movement stopped. Dismissing it as the wind, he got back to work. But the tarp began to move again and the movement seemed more intentional. Along the wall beside him was a shovel and Reverend picked it up and banged on the side of the truck until finally the rat that had cozied itself up poked its head out at the end of the bed and leaped to the floor of the garage. Then with a bit more encouragement from Reverend's banging shovel, it took off into the night. Reverend banged a few more times on the side of the truck to encourage anything else that might be breathing underneath to come out. When nothing did, he made his way to the other side of the tarp, untying it and throwing it back.

"Well, what in the world...?"

The truck bed was empty. There were no crates of spoiled greens or freezer bags of meat. It was empty. The only thing inside was another tarp lining the bed. But Reverend was certain being this close to the truck that the smell was coming from it. He took a look around the truck thinking maybe the rat had dragged something in with it, but he found nothing.

The only other thing he could think of was that the smell was coming from the basement. He made his way back to the door and turned the handle. It was, thank God, unlocked. He stepped cautiously in. He heard a banging at the top of the basement steps.

"Whoever you are, I've called the police. You hear? You need to be gone—now!" came a light but firm voice from behind the stair door.

"It's me, Ms. Kitty," he called up the stairs. "It's Reverend Madison."

"Reverend? What's going on down there?

The stench was thicker now. He pulled the collar of his coat over his nose. Reverend found the light switch on the wall next to the door, and this time when he flicked the switch, a light came on in the middle of the room. The light was dim and it hung over a large metal table.

"Reverend?"

Too stunned to answer, Reverend stared at the large table. A table not unlike ones he had seen in the coroner's office. His feet, numb from all of the cold, were having difficulty keeping his trembling legs up as he slowly pushed his way across the floor. The basement didn't have the expected mildew smell, but instead the smell of an embalming room which he had become accustomed to in his pastoral duties. His thoughts were everywhere.

"Reverend?"

He looked up at the shelves beside it and walked over, peering into one of the many jars lined across the wall. There were eyes staring back at him. Not one or two, but jarfuls.

The thumping he'd heard earlier began again. But it was clearer and it sounded like more than one thing bumping. And it was coming from a door across the room.

"My God, Gunther, what… what have you been doing?"

He'd left the thumping behind before and he didn't see a need to do anything different. At the bottom of the steps he called up to Ms. Kitty.

"Put on your coat. I'll meet you at the top of the drive. We need to leave!"

And just as he was about to turn around, it was then that he saw them. Peeping out through closed eyes from underneath the open stairs was a man in a pair of worn out red sneakers.

And propped up against him, with eyes wide open, was the lifeless body of the witness, Kevin Kelley, in his pinstripe suit and bowler hat.

They left so quickly that Ms. Kitty hadn't taken the time to let him know that she had indeed called the police. But she hadn't seen any flashing lights coming their way as they sped away from the cul-de-sac so she thought no more of it as she held on tightly to the door handle.

The thunder, with great command, blew apart the town square's treasured maple wood tree which had stood since Becoming's inception. Reverend, his hands tightly gripping the steering wheel and his face pressed forward as he struggled to see past the wash of rain on the windshield, was so distracted that he never even noticed the shaking of the ground, not even when the tree began falling or when it hit the road missing his speeding Cadillac by less than an inch.

Had it not been for Ms. Kitty gasping and then calling out the name Jesus, he would have missed the red light. And he would have missed the green one had it not been for the blare of the car horn behind him.

It was then he noticed Ms. Kitty nervously tugging and tapping at the hem of her jacket. "Has Gunther died?" she kept asking. "What happened?" And then, out of nowhere she said, "You him, ain't you? You one of them boys. I knew it before I got in the car with you the first time. But now I'm sure."

Meanwhile, when the tree hit the ground it shook the town with such force that a hairline crack began to rise from the left hand corner of Hattie Mae's picture window. It pushed itself onward and upward until it too blew apart. It was so loud it caused Hattie Mae to bolt upright in her chair. She had spent the last several months sniffing and breathless waiting for the next thing to happen—the next bead to roll. And then she saw it. What had been hidden in plain sight. Another pearl just across the driveway inside the garage of Gunther Ferguson.

A BOOK NO LONGER CLOSED

Reverend arrived at Promisekeepers in a state of terror, sweating under his soaked spring coat, heart racing, hands shaking. He cried out for Cooke in every room, his voice loud and full of cracks. Before driving all the way to the hospital, he wanted to make sure Cooke wasn't still at the church checking on things. Still tugging at the hem of her sweater, Ms. Kitty waited in the car.

Born with a purpose. Born with a purpose. Less than twenty-four hours ago, the most difficult thing he had to deal with was writing a sermon, convincing himself and others that everyone was born to a purpose. And God's plans would ultimately win out. What bullshit!

Had Gunther been caring for the homeless simply as a predator casing his victims? What had Cooke done to Gunther—said to him—to turn him into another version of him.

"Cooke!" There was a light on in the basement apartment. "Cooke! Come out here! Now! We gotta talk." Reverend followed his voice into the room. His head cocked to the side listening for a response. His hands partially clenched, he searched every space behind each divider. Convinced he was nowhere to be found in the church, he headed towards the door. And then he saw it. Slowly, in disbelief, he walked over to the couch and sat down in front of it.

Reverend was leaning again. But this time, into things that until now were unknown to him. Sitting on Cooke's sofa, elbow to knee, he struggled to connect the memories of their combined past with the photos in the album that Cooke had left open on the table.

The story he thought he knew. It was the story of the woman and boy in the photo in his desk drawer—the photo in Ruth's hand. It was a fifty-eight year old story. A lie. And as he looked down at the album he realized the story had always been told by Cooke. He was the creator of the story that Reverend had believed for so long. Not once had Reverend questioned the story. Never asked if the beginning, middle or end were true. Why had that been? Cooke had reminded him over and over again why they had fled Becoming and why it wouldn't be a good idea to return too soon.

"Carl, Jr. let's go, man! Didn't you hear what I said?!"

At eighteen years of age Carl stood in the middle of his grandmother's kitchen trying to understand the "hurry up" in his cousin's voice.

"They got guns, man! I didn't say we need to think about leaving, I said we are leaving and that's that."

Winter pants and spring shirts. One blue sock with a white stripe and one black dress sock. Pictures with no frame and no album and lidless bottles of blue and clear liquids. Cooke was packing Carl's suitcase the way he cooked. A little bit of this and a nip and a dash of that. If they indeed were going to flee, Carl wished that Cooke would get his own suitcase and leave his things alone. Besides, he had only been in town for a week and a half. He hadn't even finished unpacking yet. But that didn't matter now. Angry men with guns were on there way down the road. Carl had done something bad. The worst thing he'd ever done. But it had happened after the drink Cooke had given him. Cooke had warned him that drinking was for grown men who knew how to handle themselves. But he thought he was. And he thought he could. So he drank. And he told Hazel she could drink too. Encouraged her even. His beautiful, beautiful Hazel. Whatever the bad thing was, he had done it to her. Had to. Everyone of those men carrying a gun was a man that belonged to her. A father, a cousin, an uncle. They all belonged to her. But they all knew him, too. And just twelve or so hours ago they were telling him how glad they were that he was going to be a part of their family. They knew he wouldn't do anything to hurt her. He loved her. Couldn't think of anyone or anything he loved more. Didn't they know that? But Cooke said they were coming with guns, and there was no time to spare. There wouldn't be any talking. Cooke said he had seen angry men like this before. "Once they get it in their heads they been wronged," he'd said, "and start talking together about how they been wronged, men usually go out to seek justice." And even then, Carl knew justice never had room for talking.

Round and round in his head went the memories of that day. If only he'd known that, when walked across, lies were just like gravel. They creep up into the dark crevices of your soul and become a permanent thing. If only he'd known that the dirt they thought they were leaving behind in the city limits of Becoming would be tracked away with them, they might have changed their shoes.

But he didn't. And with every ensuing day, month and year spent away from Becoming walking across more impervious creeping things, by the time they returned, his soul was filled. Every deep dark crack and crevice, clogged. So much so till he could no longer contain those impervious things. And so now they were flying out. And now were filling all the air around him like birds flyin' out a cage.

Until he'd taken the pastorate at Promisekeepers, he'd never returned to Becoming. But now, looking down into the pages of Cooke's photo album he realized that Cooke hadn't taken his own advice. The book was filled with pictures of Cooke in Becoming. Pictures of him and her—and the boy. The boy in his arms, the boy propped on this knee, the boy playing ball, the boy, the boy. The woman Hazel that Reverend had loved so deeply, and her boy—their boy—Gunther.

THE BEGINNING OF TRUTH

Suddenly Reverend appeared in the doorway of the family waiting room looking beaten and worn. Kitty stood beside him looking a bit shaken.

"Reverend!" Ruth rushed to him. "What in God's name happened to you!"

Julia, Ruth and Cooke had been sitting silently in the room involved in their thoughts when the two entered. Cooke got up from his chair and walked towards Reverend. Reverend's appearance made him ask, "Were you at Gunther's? Why are there p-p-police at his house?"

Reverend's response was sharp. "You never left Becoming, did you?"

Cooke shot a look over at Kitty and then back to Reverend.

"Listen, I'm not sure what you're ta-talkin' bout, but I just drove by Gunther's on the way back here and the street is filled with police cars. Weren't you just there? Do you know what's happening?"

And even though Ruth's first priority was to get Reverend

some attention, she waited to hear the answer. Her hand wrapped around the picture frame in her coat pocket.

"Yeah, I was there. But I took a detour on the way back. I just came from your place looking for you. I saw it, Cooke. All laid out on the table in your apartment. The photo album with pictures of you, and her… and him!"

Ruth was frightened. She'd never seen her husband so angry. His fists were balled up beside him and his teeth were clenched.

"Carl, baby, you're scaring me. We need to get you down to emergency and see if you're okay."

I'm not going anywhere right now!"

"Well, if you won't go, I'm not leaving you." She looked at Cooke. "What's going on?"

Reverend yanked Cooke by the arm across the room.

"There are bodies in Gunther's basement," he whispered.

"What do you mean there's bodies in his basement? I don't know nu'thin' about bodies in Gunther's basement."

"Don't you lie to me, Cooke. Don't tell me you don't know anything about them. I was there. I saw 'em with my own eyes. And one of them…"

"One of them what?" Beads of sweat were beginning to form on Cooke's forehead.

Reverend moved closer to Cooke's ear. "One of 'em is Kevin Kelley!" He pulled the ring from his pocket and shoved it into Cooke's hand. As he stepped back away from Cooke, he said, "I know you had somethin' to do with this." Reverend punched at the air. "Tell me the truth. What did you do?" His eyes were pleading and his voice was shaking."

Cooke stepped back in disbelief. "That can't be."

"Well, it damn sure is!"

Cooke felt Julia's eyes on him from a far corner. He glanced briefly and saw her eating a piece of a chocolate bar, slipping what looked to him like a wallet down into her pocket.

"It can't be. He was at the church." Cooke held his head in his hands. "He came to see me. I left him at the church."

"Where? In the kitchen?"

"No."

"Stop staring at me and tell me. Tell it!"

"I put him in the storage unit behind the building." There was a look of defeat on his face.

"Why was he in the storage unit, Cooke? What the hell was he doin' in the…"

"Reverend…" Ruth entered their space.

"Not now, Ruth."

"But look at you!"

He looked down at his muddied clothes and bloodied hands. "It's not as bad as it looks. I tripped at Gunther's. But… Ruth, I can't talk about it now. I need you to go back out so I can finish talking to Cooke. When I'm done I'll be out."

Against her best judgment, she backed away. Cooke was now looking past Reverend, his eyes full of fear. Reverend looked over his shoulder to see what Cooke was staring at. Two officers were standing at the reception desk and one was looking over at them.

"Moses! You better start talkin' and you better start talkin' fast."

"You ain't called me by my Christian name for a long time," replied Cooke wistfully.

Cooke turned away from Carl and quietly stared out of the hospital window for a brief moment. Finally, he turned. "You better sit down. There's a lot to t-t-tell. And I imagine when I'm through, you'll be happy to see those policemen haul my ass outta here."

WHERE IT ALL BEGAN

THE OUTDOOR MAN

With both arms tucked snugly between chest and thigh, three-year-old Moses squatted in the plot of dirt at the bottom of his grandmother's front porch steps staring out at the silhouettes moving beyond him in the twilight. Like fireflies, they weaved through the evening air, some settling under trees with legs splayed and others disappearing through the loosely hinged doors of Momma O's barn.

"Where do they disappear to?" he'd asked Momma O one night. She looked out into the night but never answered.

At three years old, it was easy for him to imagine the figures melting into the ground like spring snow, giving room for new ones to rise up in the fresh hazy light of morning. Even though his grandmother assured him that people could not simply melt into the ground, and even though he believed that Momma O never told him anything that wasn't right, he still had a hard time feeling certain of their comings and goings. New ones showed up almost every morning with hands open wide to receive whatever food or drink Momma O could spare.

Offering "bless you's" and "thank you, ma'am's" in return. Then throughout the day, he would catch glimpses of them stacking wood or mending a fence post. And then as now, dusk would crawl in to meet them and by the next morning some of them would be gone, and new ones would arrive to replace them.

"Come on up here, boy," Momma O called. "It's time for you to be thinking about going to sleep." Momma O patted her thigh and motioned for him to come. Moses turned his head and squinted at her through the light of the setting sun. The floorboards moaned as she pushed herself lazily back and forth in the porch swing to the sound of the Platters singing "The Great Pretender" on the radio inside. One of the best times of the day was lying in her lap slowly being lulled to sleep by the rhythmic movement and familiar sounds. On any other given evening, he would have already taken his place beside her. But the day had brought with it many irregularities and he was having a difficult time adjusting.

"Moses, do what I tell you, now." Her voice was stern but not angry.

"Yessum," he replied, dragging himself up the three steps and letting her help him into her lap. The dusting of red powder that he had never seen her use before was all but gone from her cheeks suggesting that things might soon get back to normal. It had been a long day. A confusing day. Things had happened that he didn't understand even when Momma O had answered all his questions which had started as soon as she had closed the back door on the morning's outreached hands.

"This cake ain't for sale, baby. It's for your momma's wedding day, Moses. Your momma's gettin' married today. Ain't

you been paying attention?" Momma O was a thin woman, her skin dark and leathery. She had a thick, black scar that ran down from her hairline across her left eye. Moses never asked her about it even though he spent a lot of time contemplating it. She stood with one hand on her hip and the other pointing a wooden spoon at him like she often did when she was trying to teach him something or explain something he was having a hard time understanding, like at that moment.

He was in the middle of dunkin' a biscuit in a pool of syrup so it took a minute for the next question to come to him. "What's married?"

Momma O turned her back to him and went back to stirring cake batter. "She done got you a daddy, Moses. And it's all gonna be official today."

Upon remembering the cake, Moses pulled one hand from its nesting armpit and searched its pores and creases for any hint of remaining lemon buttercream icing. He stuck his two middle fingers into pursed lips only to confirm that his fingers had been sucked bone clean. His disappointment was as deep as when he'd done it ten minutes before.

A few feet away from him standing beside the propped open screen door stood his mother. Of all the things he'd seen in his three years, he'd never seen anything as pretty as her. Her dark hair was wavy and fell soft around her shoulders. She still had on the special flowered dress with her new blue shoes he'd been warned all day not to brush up against for fear he might ruin them. The dress and the shoes seemed to make her happy, so he relented. On a day he needed her the most they had kept her away from him.

Behind her on the opposite side of the porch stood Mr. Johnson. Although he didn't understand the details of it, he was certain Mr. Johnson was the cause of the tension he felt so strongly in the air today and for some days prior. There wasn't a time he could remember before today that his mother and Momma O used voices with each other that made him scared to move. Momma O assured him once that what was going on between her and his mother had nothing to do with him, but he'd heard Momma O use the words "that boy" more than once. He was certain "that boy" had to be him because he was the only boy around. Just like when she used the words "that man." He knew she was speaking about Mr. Johnson because he was the only man in the house. And, the angry words didn't start until Mr. Johnson came. While Momma O never said the words out loud where he could hear them, he knew how she felt about Mr. Johnson. And it confirmed his feelings. He didn't much like Mr. Johnson either. He didn't like the way he felt unimportant when Mr. Johnson looked at him. He didn't like how Mr. Johnson had skin like the white people in town who called Momma O Black Olive cause she was darker than tar. And even though Mr. Johnson's skin was almost exactly like his momma's it somehow seemed important to him in a way he never noticed with his mother. But his momma's skin was his momma's. For all of the things he didn't like about Mr. Johnson, the thing he disliked the most was the way Mr. Johnson was stealing his momma away from him.

Moses remembered the first day he met Mr. Johnson. He didn't walk in like the others with no shoes and a gunny sack over his shoulder. And he hadn't melted into the ground like the others did either. No. He and his mother had been sitting on the steps pickin' green beans when Mr. Johnson pulled up to Momma O's front porch in a shiny black car that had no roof. A bowler hat was pulled down low on his forehead and his suit was covered in dust. "Ma'am?" he'd asked, "how are you with directions? Been driving for a while and I guess I done got lost," he said followed by a nervous laugh.

Moses didn't know how to tell time, but he knew Mr. Johnson had now been lost for a long stretch of it. Momma O offered him the sofa that night so he could be rested before he got on his way. But he never did get back on his way. Every morning he got up he would find Mr. Johnson asleep on the living room sofa that only company was allowed to sit on. He showed up to mealtimes, eating at the table with them instead of with the other outdoor folk. Momma O used to never allow that. After a while, his mother told him to call Mr. Johnson, Uncle Carl.

"Is he a relative, Momma?"

"Not yet, baby, but let's hope he will be soon."

Resentment of Mr. Johnson—the outdoor man that came inside—came fairly quickly for Moses. At some point, and Moses wasn't sure when, he decided he didn't quite like all the time Mr. Johnson was spending with his mother that didn't include him. He was putting his momma in his shiny black car and telling Moses they were going on something called a date and that they would be back soon. But that was only partially true. Momma O always had to put him to bed when Mr. Johnson said that, and putting him to bed had always been his mother's job. And when Moses would ask them questions about where they went or what they were doing, Mr. Johnson would always tell him to mind his own business and remember his place. He never understood what place Mr. Johnson was talking about. Every place here on Momma O's farm was his place—except for the living room sofa. His mother used to explain everything to him. But that stopped weeks ago. Now, just like Mr. Johnson, she was telling him to mind his place and he didn't much like that at all. And then to top it all off today, on a day he really found confusing, she spent all of her time with Mr. Johnson, smiling and laughing and kissing—and shooing him away.

The heaviness of his eyes and spirit gave way to an appreciation that this day was coming to an end. He would willingly mind his place and listen with his eyes closed to hear if his name were called.

"I'll be back for him, Momma. Just as soon as we get settled. And it shouldn't be too long—right Mr. Johnson?" Mr. Johnson shuffled his feet and tugged at his hat. "Momma, he's already got some things moving in Chicago, so all we got to do is find a place to live. I promise it won't be long."

"We need to get moving if we gonna make that train, baby," said Mister Johnson.

"Momma?"

Moses' eyes flickered open for the last time before giving in to sleep. His mother's pretty face looked sadder than Moses could ever remember, but he was so tired. The rhythm of the moaning floor and the patting of his thigh by Momma O had done him in. So he didn't protest when his mother walked off the porch and got into Mr. Johnson's brand new 1951 Ford Deluxe without a hug or a kiss. And he didn't ask her where she was going before his breathing fell in time to Momma O's patting. Later, he would wish he'd been awake to get that hug and kiss. Particularly a few years later when Momma O told him his mother would never be back because she got sick getting his new house ready and went on to heaven to be with the Lord. This Lord, the one the preacher talked about every Sunday morning, eventually grew to be more of a focus of hate than Mr. Johnson. At least Mr. Johnson would bring his mother home. The good Lord never did.

COMPANY'S COMIN'

Cooke, who had long shed his Christian name Moses for one he thought better suited him, banged through the kitchen door with a force that shook the pots hanging on the wall.

"Momma O! I'm b-b-back, Momma O!" he hollered, his voice bouncing off the walls like a loose ball in a tiny room.

From the far end of the kitchen, Momma O emerged, her limp pronounced, the result of a stroke four years back that left one arm dangling at her side. "Boy, what I done told you about all that hollering up in here!" she snapped, narrowing her eyes. "You must've done seen that young gal you so crazy about. You always get worked up when you see her."

"How come you always call her that g-g-gal?" Cooke's voice softened, his excitement deflating slightly. "She got a name. Her name is Hazel."

Momma O frowned, the lines on her face deepening. "Don't make no difference what her name is. If her name was John, you'd still be worked up every time you seen her. Mind what I told you. Calm down so you can stop all that stutterin'."

Cooke's face grew serious, his movements more deliberate as he carefully placed the groceries on the counter. "Besides, she ain't thinkin' about me. She ain't interested in someone black as me." The pound of sugar fell hard from his hands onto the counter, nearly toppling into the dishwater.

"Boy, you be careful with them groceries," Momma O scolded, moving closer. "We didn't hardly have enough to pay for 'em and here you are washing the sugar down the drain."

Cooke looked up, his eyes pleading for understanding. "I got everything I need for the cake, 'cept they didn't have any more vanilla so I got two fresh lemons for a lemon glaze." He held up the lemons, one in each hand like he was displaying prized possessions. Momma O softened, but only slightly. "When they comin'?"

"They'll be here on the noon train," she replied, her tone less sharp but still guarded.

Cooke leaned against the counter, shifting his weight from left to right as he pondered the upcoming visit. "Momma O, how come you ain't excited? Don't you wanna see your d-d-daughter? Tell me about her again, Momma O."

"Boy, I done told you fifty times about her. That's enough now. You'll see her for yourself in a few hours and you can ask her all the questions you want."

"But I still don't understand how I can be sixteen, almost a grown man, and just be hearing about my dead momma having a sister. And I g-got me a cousin. I ain't never had nobody else but you. But I got a real male cousin. Just like me! It's exciting!"

Momma O's gaze softened a fraction, but her voice remained firm. "First of all, you ain't near being a grown anything yet. You still got a while to go. And second of all, I doubt he's just like you. City folk are different than us out here in the country. And third of all, I'm sorry you got stuck with just me."

Cooke quickly crossed the room and wrapped his arms around her from behind, kissing her on the neck. "Aww, you know I didn't mean nothin' by that. You know I d-d-didn't. If I only had you and nobody else ever, I'd still have more than anybody I know. I love you, Momma O."

She gently shook herself free and swatted at his hands. "Go on now, you got stuff to do."

As Cooke resumed his tasks, his thoughts wandered. "Did I ever meet her before, like when I was a baby? Did she come here to see me when I was born?"

"Stop asking silly questions, boy," Momma O huffed. "You bout to get on my nerves."

"Momma O, these ain't silly questions. You told me they was twins—my auntie and my mother. I hear that twins are supposed to be closer than regular brothers and sisters. They have some kind of secret language and all that. Well, if that's so, I just don't understand how I ain't never met her. Seems like a long time not to come see your closer than normal, dead sister's son."

A gentle tapping on the back door interrupted them.

"Go on now, I done tol' ya!" yelled Cooke. "I got company comin' and I can't be feeding all y'all beggin' folks today!"

"Moses!" Momma O's voice turned real, real quick. "I done tol' you about talkin' to those folks like that! They come here cause I allow them to. I feed them because it's my callin' to take care of 'em. Somebody gotta care about people down on their luck. If you come by trouble when you growed up, I would want

somebody to help you. I don't ever wanna hear you being so rude to them again. You hear me? Well, do ya?"

"Yes, ma'am, I hear you, but I can't spend my whole life takin' care of folks who can't take care of themselves, and I ain't never gonna be one of 'em. Besides, there's other places around here they could go. Why they always got to come here?"

"Because here is where they supposed to be. I'm tired of explainin' it to you. The Lord gives everybody a job, and this here is mine."

"Well, it ain't mine," Cooke muttered under his breath, though he knew better than to say it too loud.

"You watch your mouth now. I ain't so old I can't get after you." Momma O moved over to the pantry and pulled out two of her pre-stuffed bags and handed them to the outstretched hands at the door.

....

The piece of hard candy that had been given to Carl Jr. to stave off his hunger by one of the two gray-haired wrinkled sisters that sat across from him was close to being gone. He'd held it under his tongue for safekeeping throughout the ride, managing to make it last nearly two hours. His mother had spent the entirety of the train ride crossing and uncrossing her legs, folding and unfolding her hands. At one point, he'd rested his hand on hers to try and calm her, but she was having none of that. She gently pushed his thirteen-year-old hand away and went back to her anxious routine.

"Momma? What you so worried about?" Carl Jr. asked, his eyes searching her face. He couldn't understand why his father had volunteered for the war, leaving them alone, and now, leav-

ing them alone for good. When the army men came to the door, his mother began crying before she even opened it. She just kept crying, "Lord, what are we gonna do now? What are we gonna do, Lord?" He had been confused at first, but soon, he found himself crying too.

When they finally reached Becoming, Carl was mesmerized by the relaxed, self-assuredness of the sea of Black bodies moving in and out of store doorways, up and down stairs. Driving through the streets, walking on the sidewalks. He looked and looked, and when he didn't see any White folks, he turned to his mother. "Where are all the White folks?"

She had forgotten herself what it was like to live in a place where you were just a person—not a Black person. "There are no Whites in Becoming, Carl. I thought I told you that."

"No. If you'd told me that, I would've remembered. How can that be though—no Whites, I mean?" he stammered. "I thought they were everywhere. Owned everything."

"Well, maybe everything somewhere else, but not in Becoming. Becoming is an all-Black town. There used to be a lot of them, but..."

"But what?"

"But nothin'. There just aren't any others anymore. At least not that I know of."

Two blocks up, they were able to get a taxi and headed out to the farm.

....

Moses was standing inside the screen door, staring out at the two people exiting the cab.

"You didn't t-t-tell me they was w-white, Momma O," he

said, his voice low.

Momma O got up from her chair and stood beside Moses, looking out the door. "Boy, don't be foolish. They ain't White. Just light-skinned is all. Go on out there and help them in with their bags."

Moses looked at his arm, at Momma O's face, and then down at the two faces looking up at the house from the driveway. "They's white," he mumbled.

"Shut up, boy, and go greet your cousin." Momma O ordered, standing staunchly, her voice low and giving him a little shove. Moses reluctantly stepped onto the porch.

"Hey." Moses eyed the younger boy in front of him with caution and much curiosity.

"Hey."

"I'm Moses. But I like to go by the name I give myself. Cooke."

"You gave yourself that name?"

"Yup. Sure did. Think it suits me better. I ain't tryin' to cross the Red Sea, just be a good cook."

"It never occurred to me you could name yourself. I'm Carl, Junior." His smile was as shiny as the shoes he wore.

"I reckon you are." Moses stared for a few more seconds before adding, "Y'all late."

"The train got held up," replied Carl excitedly. A big ol' truck was stuck on the track and they had to get a group of men to move it outta the way. You should've seen it. Never saw nothing like that in my life."

"Did you help, too?" asked Moses growing cautiously interested.

"No. Momma didn't want me to get my suit dirty. Only bought

the one."

"Can't imagine you even needing the one. Least not out here."

Carl took a step back and grabbed his mother's arm. "This here is my momma."

"Momma O told me you and my mother were twins," said Cooke taking one step down and longing for some sense of familiarity.

"Yeah?" Until now, she had gone unnoticed. She squeezed her son's hand hard and he tried to pull away which only made her squeeze harder. Finally, he seemed to give in, but she still couldn't seem to loosen her grip. "What else did she tell you?" she asked sheepishly glancing over at Momma O.

"Not much. Do you look exactly like my momma? There weren't ever any pictures of her, so I never knew what she looked like—least not till now."

"I reckon I do. That's what being a twin means I guess."

"I knew she was pretty. I just had a feelin'," responded Moses quietly.

"Wanna go fishing?" asked Cooke feeling a need to change the subject.

Carl turned to his mother, "May I?"

"Well, you can't go fishing in that suit," she replied, jabbing him playfully on his shoulder.

"Moses," ordered Momma O, "go show your cousin his room so he can change and y'all can get to going. There's only a few hours left before dinner time, and you promised a basketful of fish for dinner."

Cooke lowered his voice as if sharing a secret. "Momma O doesn't much like me changing my name to Cooke. Can't seem to get her to call me Cooke even when we ain't in church."

"Quit being smart boy and get going."

The lake in Becoming was clear and full of many kinds of fish. Bass. Catfish. For most of the first part of their visit, the two boys spent their time fishing and talking about the differences between the city and the country. And for Cooke, trying to make peace with his cousins's complexion.

A FINE BUCKET OF FISH

A week passed and the two boys got into a rhythm of chores and fishing. Cooke was pleasantly surprised at how quickly his newfound cousin took to country life. To his delight, Carl Junior eagerly wanted to learn how to gather eggs and milk the cows—chores he was yearning to be free from. And in the short week, Carl was catching as many fish as his teacher, proudly bringing them home for Momma O to fry up for supper. Carl's eagerness to be more like his now mentor quickly pushed aside the differences between them that Cooke initially felt so deeply.

"I thought you had it!"

"How could I have it? Do you see anything in my hands?" retorted Cooke.

"Well, you don't see anything in mine either, do ya?"

"Never mind all that," said Cooke, waving his hand in frustration. "I'll go get the bait. I don't know how you thought we were going fishing with no bait."

"No, I can go."

"No. I can take the shortcut and be back faster. You just sit

here and wait. Be looking out there," he said pointing at the lake, "and spot us something to go after when I get back."

As Cooke took off running,

Carl picked up a handful of stones and sat down by the water's edge, tossing them gently into the lake.

"And stop throwing rocks in the water!" Cooke called over his shoulder. "You're gonna scare the fish off, and then what we gonna do?!"

As the house came into Cooke's view, he spotted the bait box from across the yard and couldn't imagine how he'd forgotten it. Taking the porch steps two by two, he reached for the box. Through an open window, behind a wind blown curtain, the voices of his aunt and Momma O battered the stillness of the Sunday afternoon.

"What did you think I was goin' to tell him? That his white-lookin' momma walked off with his white-looking stepdaddy to go make white-looking babies and they didn't want him dirtin' up their passin' family? I wasn't gonna be the one to tell him that. No. You dead. You hear me! You dead. You dead to him and you dead to me."

"Momma..."

"Don't Momma me. You didn't want him and you didn't want me. But we doin' fine without you and the rest of the mess you made. He don't want you no more and I don't want you either. So, you can go back to wherever it is you came from with that boy of yours, and I don't never need you to come back."

"Momma, I don't have anywhere else to go. And besides, that boy is your grandson too."

"Nowhere else to go? Humph! You had plenty of places to

go when you left here thirteen years ago! You said you was coming back for that boy. Instead, you go off and have another one so you don't need him anymore. Too black for you, wasn't he, with that high yella negro you left out of here with. And then I have to spin a lie so's not to hurt him. And then you make me have to tell another lie cause you wanna come back. Twin sister. You lied to him enough when you told him you was comin' back. And now you starting a whole new lie. I don't need you here. We've done just fine without you. He's a happy kid. He's a fine kid. He's a good kid. He don't need you here. Tomorrow morning, you need to figure out where to go, cause I want you gone. You hear! I want you back outta this house!"

"But Momma, ... I thought we'd stay a while so Carl can get to know Moses," she pleaded.

"Why? So he can leave him too? No!"

"But Momma, they're brothers. They should know each other. Pretty soon they're gonna be all they have."

Moses peeked into the window just in time to see Momma O move a nose length away from her daughter and stick her finger in her face. "You say one thing to that boy to hurt him again, and you gonna wish you was dead." With that, Momma O turned on her heel and headed to see who was knocking at the kitchen door.

It was dinner, and the air around the table was tense. Momma O hadn't said two words to her daughter and Cooke hadn't said much more to Carl. Whether it was true or not, it seemed to Cooke that there were more people than usual knockin' on the back door that evening. The last one to knock was a light-skinned fella. Almost as light as Carl. And it was then that something happened inside Cooke. The enemy had always been outside of them—he and Momma O. Calling them names for the color of their skin as if it was something they could take on and off. As if the darkness or brightness of skin had anything at all to do with the person inside of it. But now the enemy was inside. A white looking momma turned aunt cause she couldn't abide a black child. A white cousin turned brother who had all the advantages and mothering Cooke hadn't been allowed. And now this damn near white hand standing at the back door asking him to give up his Momma O. It all churned in his head as he washed the dishes. It churned in his head as he told his grandmother goodnight. And it would churn in his head later as the barn and every high yella thing in it burned down to the ground.

ONE DOWN, ONE TO GO

The falling was slow but brief, begun as the interlude to Cooke's dramatic storytelling. The pinging sound of the elevator, the quiet chatter of waiting families—the sounds all seemed to evaporate into thin air. With each backward, feathery inch Reverend surrendered, sliding into a black abyss, falling until he was one with it. A few more inches and he let his jaw drop, and out of his mouth they flew—one blood pecking bird after another pushing and shoving to get out with as much determination as they'd had to get in, and going up in smoke with the quickness of a magician's flash paper. And though he couldn't see them, he knew his hands were clean again. A few more inches and Reverend closed his eyes, and when he hit the ground, he was dead.

THE COUNT

Later when people would ask, Hattie would say that it had been the particular shade of gray in the rainclouds and the size of the recent raindrops that had been the clue. It all pointed to something extraordinary that was coming. The rain had just been the prelude. And she was right.

While many had joined the scene, she'd been standing in the same spot for hours under a clear vinyl umbrella tapping her foot in a widening puddle as she rolled her beads and hummed quietly. Close enough to hear everything but not close enough to be noticed, she heard every word whispered amongst the police officers.

Fifteen bodies floating in rainwater in a basement cavern, wrapped as mummies, knees to chest, had been carried out and were stacked one on top of the other in a refrigerated truck parked in the driveway of Gunther Ferguson. But that wasn't all of it.

Just as they had begun replacing her cracked window, she'd moved her chair over to a second window facing the Fergusons with a better view of the backyard. She had gotten a bean wedged in a back tooth and had been picking at it with the tip of a nail file when she saw the first flashing lights parking in front of the Fergusons' drive. She pulled in closer to the window, her nose just brushing the sheer curtains, her mouth widening to get better access to the offending bean, her fingers digging furiously. When it finally popped, she jumped from her chair and scurried to the coat closet. Surely a police car was something that would warrant her going outside to see about.

By the time she made it outside, there was an ambulance, another police car and then another. When her feet first touched the edge of the Fergusons' drive, she overheard the first officer, a little brown-skinned, twenty-six-year-old man whose wife frequented the Sunshine Motel on the outskirts of town when her husband worked the nightshift, saying to the second officer that the garage door had been open when he arrived. He thought he recognized the smell coming from inside. And since no one answered the ringing of the front or back bells, he made his way in. And sure enough, because his nose never failed him, he found a body inside a vat filled with some kind of powder. Epsom salts, maybe?

When they made their way back into the basement, Hattie Mae had moved further down the drive, standing just on the grassy edge, mostly unnoticed. It was only the Chief, who was always cordial to her when passing on the street, that approached her to ask if she knew who had been at the house since Mr. Ferguson was lying in a hospital bed. It was only the calling of the first officer to the Chief to say that two more bodies had been found under the stairs that saved her from having to admit to him that she did not know who had been at the house. That she had been derelict in her duty. So there were the first three bodies.

Soon the Chief was calling out to the second officer to put in a call for the coroner and the FBI.

"How do I call the FBI?" the officer asked innocently. "We ain't never had to call for the FBI before."

"Just call dispatch," the Chief snapped back. "Tell 'em we might have a mass murder on our hands out here! And get Mike Langford out here."

"What we need a locksmith for this hour of the night, Chief?"

"We got a locked door back here we can't find a key to. There's a banging noise comin' from behind it. Could be somebody trapped in there."

And it wasn't long before Mike Langford was walking down the drive past the police cars and the gathering crowd to unlock a door. Hattie was sure it was him she heard just moments later crying out, "God almighty! What in man's hell?!" And out from the basement and through the garage came a gush of water like the breaking of water in childbirth.

When the coroner would finally arrive, Hattie Mae listened as the Chief explained to her about the three bodies found in a basement set up for mummification with vats of this and vats of that. And jars. Jars of soft tissue things like eyes. He had never seen eyes outside of a head before.

The horror of it all, the Chief said, was behind the door Mike Langford had unlocked. There were mummies. Some had been floating in water that was pouring into the room from a crack in the ceiling and had floated out when he opened the door. But there were so many more. There were shelves full of them in wooden boxes. How many? Maybe a hundred. Maybe hundreds. He hadn't begun the count, but he was sure there were at least a hundred.

Hattie Mae was astonished. Clearly, Mr. Ferguson had been much more clever than his mother. Burying the bodies in the basement instead of the yard. When the police chief said they also needed to check the backyard, she nodded in agreement knowing what they would find. If they had asked, she would have been able to tell them exactly how many bodies had been dragged across the yard. Sixty-three. One body for every lilac bush—every rose bush. She had witnessed the burying of all but the first two. It was the missing of those two burials, that caused her to pull her chair up to the windows at night.

But now knowing how Mr. Ferguson had out maneuvered her, standing under her umbrella alone watching the groups of onlookers that had gathered, she wondered if she was also a part of their conversation. She wondered what the conversations would be later in the morning when people would ask if she still had the right to roll more beads or even keep the ones she had.

HOVERING 3—
HE WALKED AWAY

He knew now that the first time he met him was not the first time he'd seen him. It had been Reverend's first Sunday at Promisekeepers when Gunther met him. Reverend was walking across the parking lot, a handful of papers and Bibles in his hand. Gunther, with dirt still under his nails, was helping three people from the back of his truck. It had been Gunther's hope that the new preacher would be more welcoming than Cooke usually was at the farm. More welcoming than the city government who was always trying to find ways to get them out of Becoming. But it was not to be. Reverend looked at them like he was smelling the bottom of a sewer drain. And they felt it. When they refused to go in, Gunther sat outside with them on the church steps waiting for the end of service when they could visit the Church's pantry. That day stayed with Gunther for a long time after and shadowed every interaction he had with the new Reverend Carl Madison. And even when the Reverend agreed to open the dining room to them during the week, he couldn't just receive it as the Reverend changing his opinion about the people. Even though the Reverend was fond of him. Treated him like a son. Listened to him. And now, here in the space of everything known, he understood.

The first time he had seen Reverend was at the hospital when his mother lay dying. Just before she'd taken her last breath, she had looked at the doorway and pointed, "Your father," she'd said, "bring him to me."

At first Gunther thought she was having a death vision. But something provoked him to get up from his seat and go to the door. Looking down the hall, he saw a man rushing down the hallway. And now, as their spirits united, he realized why in body Reverend had always seemed familiar to him. He had been that man walking down the hall away from his mother's dying words.

UNRELENTING

"I remember now," said Kitty. "Those two boys that ran out of Becoming. One was from out of town and the other lived on a farm around here somewhere. That was you two, wasn't it? You better tell me and tell me quick. What happened to my sister?" Kitty stood coolly in front of Cooke who was once again seated in the family waiting room of the hospital, gently rocking himself, his wrapped finger beginning to bleed through. Ruth had ordered him to leave her sight. All of his evilness, she said, had killed her husband and left her alone. Julia, stunned by all that was happening around her, was moved by a repentant Cooke, whose tears were soaking his wrapped finger.

An unrelenting Kitty, unmoved by Cooke's current state, pressed on. "I thought I recognized you when I first arrived. It was you two, wasn't it? You two that got run out of Becoming for raping my sister."

Julia pressed herself up against the wall making sure she remained unnoticed so she could hear the whole conversation.

Kitty pulled up a chair and sat down in front of Cooke.

"Which one of you raped my sister? We ain't leaving here until you tell me what happened."

Julia quietly let go of the wallet she had been holding onto in her pocket and reached into her purse, hunting for her smudge brush.

Cooke rubbed his face with his good hand. There was so much more to tell.

THE CONCEIVING OF GUNTHER FERGUSON

Cooke watched as his car rolled easily up the drive to Momma O's house. Carl Jr., now twenty-one, was at the wheel, and sitting beside him was Hazel Beecham. Carl had met her when he'd gotten back to Becoming two weeks ago and had been obsessed with her. It was a wonder he hadn't met her on any of the other annual visits he'd made to Becoming. Cooke knew Hazel's father to be a strict man, so it was surprising that he had allowed her to go to the dance with him and Carl. Her sister Kitty devised the tale that allowed her to get away for a few hours.

Carl pushed back at the idea of picking up Hazel first and then coming back to get Cooke. But that was the only way Cooke knew to get her to the farm. So since it was his car, Cooke said it was his rules or nothing, and Carl went along with it.

Warned to be careful not to wake Momma O, whose state of health was the reason for Carl's visit, the horn blew lightly and only once when Carl returned. A few seconds later, Cooke was calling and waving to him from the door of the barn. Carl got out of the car and headed towards him.

"No, bring her too."

"For what?"

"I got us something to get started with." Cooke grinned widely and held up a bottle.

"You know I don't drink, Cooke, and she don't neither."

"Bring your sissy ass on over here and don't leave her sitting there by herself."

Reluctantly, Carl helped Hazel out of the car and across the yard.

"You not even dressed yet. I can't keep her out too long."

"Who needs a party anyway when we got all we need right here?"

"Cooke, I..."

"Oh, stop your whining. It won't take me a minute to get dressed. It's just a pair of pants and a shirt." He held out a glass to Hazel. "I got something special for you."

"Cooke, she don't drink."

"She drink tea, don't she? It's just some porch tea from yesterday. Here," he said shoving the glass at her.

Hazel looked at Carl first and then back at Cooke. "I guess a bit of tea won't hurt."

Cooke already had two water glasses of whiskey ready. He handed one to Carl. "Now don't worry about drinking all of it. It's just something to get us started for a great night." Cooke made a toast to the three of them and after watching them drink down their beverages, excused himself to put on his clothes. He stayed away about ten minutes before returning, having not changed his clothes.

Carl was passed out in a pile of hay. Hazel was sitting up against the barn wall. A crooked smile rose on Cooke's face. He walked over to Carl, leaned down and slapped his face lightly three times. He was out cold. Hazel was mumbling. He walked over and ran his hand across her hair. "What you t-talkin' bout? I got whatever it is you need, pretty Hazel. What you need?"

After a few tries she was able to say, "I gotta pee."

Cooke chuckled. "Well come on let me help you." He pulled her up off the barrel and walked her further into the barn and away from Carl. He leaned her up against one of the back walls. "Here, girl, let me help you out of those panties." Holding her up with one hand, he pushed his hand up under her dress and along the inside of her leg.

"I gotta pee bad."

Cooke pushed his body against hers to hold her up and began pulling down her panties.

"No, Carl. I can do it."

"Carl?" Cooke chuckled. "Yes, let Carl help you, baby," he whispered in her ear. "It's gonna be alright. You know Carl loves you, Hazel, right? Carl loves his Hazel."

He'd gotten her panties down just in time. He pushed her legs apart as the warm yellow liquid flowed between them. When it stopped, he guided her to the floor of the barn. As soon as her head hit the floor, she was out and Cooke unbuttoned his pants.

When he was done, Cooke stood over Hazel, fixing his clothes, tears flooding his eyes. "You thought you were too good for me, with your high yella ass." And then catching a glimpse of something beside him, he turned. Coming into the barn from the back were two of Momma O's people dragging a gunny sack. "Get outta here! What I done tole y'all! Get out!" Cooke picked up a rock and hurdled it at one of the old men. The blood it drew from his scalp didn't cause Cooke any hesitation. He ran over and yanked at the old man and threw both of them into a corner of the barn.

"I betta not hear a peek outta you, you hear," he whispered. "If I ever hear anything from you, I'll beat you senseless, you old lazy bastards!"

It had taken a lot of energy for Cooke to get Carl moved to the front yard and Hazel into the front seat of the car. As he was checking the barn to make sure he'd gotten everything cleaned up, it occurred to him that it was never good to have a witness. But the ensuing fire wasn't intentional. Knocking over the lantern truly was accidental. It was just that he hadn't come to terms with leaving a witness as the barn burned. So he left both men in there. And they didn't even make a noise.

And besides, they were beggars. Dirty, stinking, useless beggars. Like Mr. Johnson, constantly taking, taking taking. Them with their hands stuck out taking biscuits and ham—and Momma O's attention. And Mr. Johnson, taking his momma. And Carl who had everything taking the only girl he loved.

He had tried to tell Momma O, over and over again, this was her calling. Not his. Over and over again he told her. But she would just keep sayin' how they too belonged to God and how maybe Becoming was a place God created for them and that's why they came. And if he made a place for them, then he must've made people for them. "Everything and everyone has a purpose, Moses," she would say. And then he would say, "Momma O, that can't be because I ain't got one." And as the fire grew bigger and stronger his memories of those conversations grew until he convinced himself that Momma O was wrong. Sometimes things are simply what they are. And maybe those vagrants were just that and nothing more. And maybe they did come here to die, but not because of a loving father, who he never found, but just because sometimes life is what it is. If they died then or later, they were gonna die. Maybe dying in the fire was better. It certainly was faster. No more laying in the street, begging for food and not knowing where you were going to sleep at night. Maybe the plan was that there was no plan. What kind of purpose did these vagrants have? Living so that others could take care of 'em? Feed them? House them? For free?

The story Cooke told Hazel's sister Kitty involved Carl getting drunk and getting Hazel drunk. He didn't care about the lyin' at the time. It was the least of what he'd done.

The force by which Kitty hit Cooke knocked him out of the chair and onto the floor.

"You bastard! First you rape her, and then you come in and out of her life like a savior. You're that man she told me was always helping her with this and helping her with that, aren't you? She told me just how thoughtful and caring you were. What did you tell her about your precious Reverend? What lie did you tell that kept her waiting for him? Looking for him?"

"I didn't tell her anything. I just told her…"

"Told her what?!"

"I told her he might come back. That she should keep looking for him."

"Looking for him where?"

"On the streets," he said waving his hand toward the windowed wall. "She spent all of her time searching for him in the streets of Becoming."

"Why would she do that? I don't understand."

"I told her he fell on hard times and was living on the streets."

"Your lies never stopped!"

"You gotta understand. She was mine first."

HOVERING 4— THE WRAITH

As he hovered, Gunther saw the first night he followed his mother. Had she been a faster driver, he would have lost her as she drove slowly around town. But he found it easier than he had thought to keep up with her on his ten-speed bike. She never drove the highway. He certainly would have lost her if she had.

They lay crumbling around the fire. The throwaways. The lunatics. The untouchables. Crumbling yet breathing, except for the one. But breathing or no, all were expectant, and the one maybe more so than the others. The wraith, the specter, sheeted in yellow had been way overdue. Not in a regular every Thursday at noon kind of way, but in the way you feel time in your bones. Like knowing when rain is due, or knowing when something bad is going to happen just because things have been good for too long. That kind of timing. When she did come, they had formed a circle, more or less, and lay exposed near the fire like pill bugs tucked end to end. And when she came whispering, "Baby, is that you? Is that you, baby?" she was greeted by blackened fingertips that flicked at her over a turned shoulder, and cries that sent her skittering backward like a crab. From one pill bug to the next, she made her way neither encouraged nor discouraged—just dull-eyed and hopeful. She had looked everywhere—she thought. She had checked every face—she thought. And finally, she was on her way back to the truck ready to go to the next fire, the next group of pill bugs. But then, just as she pulled herself up to where the bridge met the ground, a twig snapped off into her hand and that is where she found him. Behind the twig. His mouth wide open and eyes as dull as hers. Insects, flies and all manner of crawling things had begun to make their home in the open holes in his head. His nose, his ears, his mouth, his eyes. She shooed away the bugs that had collected on his nose and mouth and stared at him for a long time. Finally, she leaned in close and whispered, "Baby is that you? Is that you, baby?" She pressed her middle and index fingers firmly against the moving hairs of his throat, unaware that it made the hairs of her arm begin to move as she waited for his answer. Cool flesh, not cold but cool, that was his answer. He was ready to go back with her. A sigh, long and easy, blew through her slightly parted lips and she closed her eyes for a moment as she said a quiet prayer of thanks to a god who was kind enough to bring her love back to her—once again. She opened her eyes and took another long look at him—not noticing that his hairline had changed, as had his skin color. And if he'd been standing she might have noticed that this time he was much shorter. "I'll be back," she whispered in his ear just as the slimy white thing that had begun to climb out of it reversed its direction. She headed back the way she had come and in less than three minutes was reaching out to open the door of her red Ford truck. She had parked it down the road behind some bushes so as not to be spotted. This not being the first time she had found him under this particular bridge, finding her way down to the water's edge in the truck without lights was less of a feat than it had been the first few times. She eased the truck up onto the road without turning on the lights and headed up towards the bridge. The road ran parallel to the water and just about a half mile past the bridge the incline between the road and the water's edge was negligible. It was there she made a hard left and slowly coasted down the embankment. Just as the wheels of the truck met the water she made another sharp left and headed back towards the bridge. When she got right below him, she turned the truck around and backed it up the incline as far as she thought safe. Then she pushed down the emergency brake. Everything else she did at this point could have been done with her eyes closed because the routine was so familiar. She slid down out of the truck's cabin and stepped quickly out of her black pumps. She dropped them behind her seat and they landed with a soft thud. Her dress was the next thing she slid out of and then her slip. She folded them both, first in thirds from side to side and then from top to bottom and carefully laid them on the passenger's seat. From under the driver's seat, she pulled a man's large-sized T-shirt and a pair of jeans. The night air on her body always slowed her down at this point. It was nice to feel caressed even if only by an unseen intangible thing. Reluctantly she got into her clothes and headed to the back of the truck. Under a canvas tarp lay a wood plank and she tugged at it until one end of it lay on the ground and the other end butted up against the edge of the truck bed. Halfway up the plank, she crawled, stopping and bouncing every so often until she was sure it would hold both their weight. Finally, she slid down and the wraith went skirring back up the hill.

That night, when he had realized she was on her way home, it had taken some riding through backyards to beat her there. But then, when in the body, he didn't think she would have noticed anyhow if he was a bit later. She was too busy dragging that dead body and burying it under the newly planted lilac bushes.

AS HEADLINES CHANGE

With mouths agape and eyes bulging, doctors and nurses stood side by side at the nurses' stations and in the halls of the hospital listening in disbelief about the horrific find in the house of the man who killed the girl at Hank's Pizzeria two nights ago. Over and over again the television stations replayed the interview.

"I cannot believe it! Dead people in his basement? Who would have guessed?" Carlita, in her television debut, stood in front of Promisekeepers Church speaking to a news reporter with one hand on her forehead and the other on her hip. She looked shocked at what she'd just been told, but happy to be the interviewee all at the same time. "I've only been working here at the church for about seven months, but he always did seem a little—well—you know, odd," she continued as if sharing a secret. "Maybe even a little creepy with those long thin fingers of his. He was a good-lookin' man though, some might even say handsome. So it seemed kinda weird to me that he wasn't married. Didn't even have a girlfriend as far as I could tell. And at his age. But you know, he was always helping out around here. Running errands. But you just never know about people, do you? And now he's dead, and how will we ever know why he did it—killed all those men? It was all men, right?"

And while Carlita talked, the camera scanned the assortment of men, and a few women, standing nearby, lined up on the side of the church. The camera landed on a woman dressed nattily standing in a pair of gold shoes.

"We believe," began Charlie Hunt of W2BT News in his deep baritone voice, "but have not yet been able to verify, that the man Gunther Ferguson, too, has died from his injuries sustained in that accident."

As the shocking news story grew into describing the more than one hundred bodies found in the cavern, and the call for an excavator from Billup's Heavy Tools and Machinery, it completely obscured the fact that the rain had stopped. Sometime between Gunther's death and the newscaster's interview, it had stopped abruptly in the early morning hours. Even when the newscaster threw it over to Ted the weatherman, Ted mentioned the reappearance of the sun so casually, and so quickly reengaged the host about the dead bodies, people wondered if three-quarter inches of rain per hour had really been as unseasonal as first claimed a week ago.

But the change in weather had not been lost on Cooke. For the longest time, he stood on the steps of the hospital looking up into the sky, blood dripping from his unattended hand. He watched as the sun crested the trees, and noticed the birds who were once again flying from one to the other as they built new nests for their soon-to-come chicks. The air no longer smelled of wet dirt, but simply clean. The townspeople would now be able to close their closet doors and get back to their normal lives.

The news of Gunther's demise had come before Cooke had even picked himself up off the floor. It was fortunate timing though as it allowed him to slip by the mourners, of which there were just two left, Julia and Kitty, and the two officers who were now waiting for new orders since the alleged murderer was dead.

Standing on the steps, the pain of Gunther's death filled Cooke like an over-inflated tire. What was there left to do? There were his own bodies to be accountable for. Kevin Kelley, the men in the barn, and the others. The others no one but he knew about.

"Hey, mister! Mister? You're bleeding."

Cooke glanced over at the little girl sitting in a wheelchair beside the exit door holding her suitcase on her lap and then down at his hand. Disappearing into the concrete step were great drops of blood whose trail he saw went past the hospital's opening doors and into the lobby. "I know," he thought. And then headed towards his car in the lot.

Emotionless and sober, Cooke sat behind the wheel of the car. "Take me outta here," he said to his car, his companion for many years. "I'll let you decide where we go."

And so he managed the brakes and the gas pedal and turned the wheel this way and that until finally he found himself on Route Six. As he looked ahead, he recognized the eastwardly looking mounds and remembered the first day he'd driven away from Becoming wondering if he'd ever return. Wondering what the world past Becoming had for him. He'd had hopes then that who he was could be changed by new places, new people, new experiences. He'd hoped that a life away from Becoming would make him the person he'd overheard Momma O talk about through the fluttering curtains on the porch that summer day. He told himself he was going away to be kind. To be good. To be loved. To be away from the judgments of his skin color, and the burning people in the barn. And the tragedy of Hazel. And today he realized with certainty that all of who he was could not be overcome by place nor time.

It wasn't until his car suddenly stopped and he realized he was out of gas, that he felt the vibrations, heard the rumblings of the mounds he was smack dab in the middle of. His first thought was that there had never been an earthquake in Becoming. So that couldn't possibly be happening. But then, just as the first pile of mud pulled away from the mound he remembered his exertion a few days ago while driving. And he remembered shouting to the unsuspecting woman to meet him in hell. And so now, he wondered if he would.

It would be more than a year before Cooke's body would be found, decomposed under the mudslide and being eaten by a multitude of slimy things. Asphyxiation is what the coroner would write on his death certificate. But Kitty and Ruth and even Julia would say the cause of death wasn't asphyxiation at all. It was just plain evil.

PLAY IT AGAIN, SAM

If only he'd known that Julia knew and just how much she had been willing to help him—had, in fact, helped him. Sending the indigent released from the hospital out to the farm so they would be easy to find. Even sending him to the back of the church where he was sure to find Kelley. And moving bodies—even though she hadn't done a very good job of hiding them—she did it for him. Things could have ended so differently.

When all was settled with Moses, he and his mother's spirits rejoiced for the work they had done together for the men. The men, the many men whom they had found in all of the empty broken places. The unloved men who died languishing under bridges and in the bush beside the roads, hungry and cold. All the men who had tried to live a life of meaning and goodness and giving only to become a stain on society. A society that had itself left them destitute. The least of these unable to overcome a society that only honored those who could keep up the pace, and punished those who couldn't—these, these were the men they took up as a cause. Because they too were human beings, subject to the love of a creator who declared all men were created by his hand, the hand of love. So even after Hazel knew, was absolutely sure Cooke was Gunther's father, she still drove her red truck through Becoming. And even though each body she met took her back to the time of looking for Gunther's father, a time when her mind was not her own, she still brought them home. Still gave them as much of a holy putting away as she could with a spray of flowers, of lilacs and roses to honor their lives, whatever they were.

And while the residents of Becoming would die believing him to be inhumane, a murderer, a gross oddity, they, the men, knew differently. And now, their faraway tinkling turned to a chorus as they sang to him the song he had so often sung to them.

"Oh, Lord will you remember me when I am called to go." Gunther smiled and turned towards the light. He was much closer.

"When I have crossed death's chilly seas, will he his love there show?" As Gunther moved towards the light the many men whom his hands had bathed, rubbed in myrrh and aloe, and wrapped in cloth—all whom he honored as divine spirits in the work of his hands, lined the way. Smiling and singing they welcomed him in.

"O, Yes! He heard my feeble cry, from bondage set me free!" And they showed him. Each one sharing their journey to Becoming. Their stories starting with all the hopes of a new day as a child, that twisted during their life journey. That wore them down. That battered them. Until they were sent to their loving brother who had been created to care for them. And who

could have left his work by the wayside and not accepted it. But didn't. A brother who took his work seriously and was determined to live a life honoring that honor.

"And when I reach death's pearly gates, he will remember me!" And he did remember them! Each one. Father Ferguson twenty-six. Father Ferguson fifty-nine. Father Ferguson sixty-five. He remembered them all. No more glasses glistening on shelves waiting to be used. No more speaking for them. Their voices were strong and clear.

And finally, with a joy, unspeakable joy, Gunther surrendered and stepped into the light.

The End

www.ingramcontent.com/pod-product-compliance
Lightning Source LLC
Chambersburg PA
CBHW060551310726
48982CB00008B/1090/J

* 9 7 9 8 9 9 9 3 8 0 1 0 4 *